Rick McQuiston

TO SEE AS A GOD SEES

Many Midnights Publishing

ISBN # 978-1-257-12274-5

Published in the United States by Many Midnights Publishing.

Cover design and artwork by Amanda (Mandy) McQuiston using Adobe Photoshop CS5.

Technical support by Walonda McQuiston, and Lori Sanborn.

Printed in the United States.

Notice: This book is a work of fiction. Any resemblance to actual persons, places, or events is purely coincidental.

Visit the author's website: many-midnights.webs.com

Email: Many_Midnights@yahoo.com

Dedicated to my wife and children.
I love you guys.

CHAPTER 1

Jerry was knocked sideways, slamming first his shoulders, and then his head into the moist stench of the pole barn walls. He frantically tried to secure his grip on something, anything strong enough to support his body weight, but continuously met with failure. His battered mind rattled with each blow into the wall.

"Leave me the hell alone!" he shouted through bloodied lips, knowing full well that the undead monstrosities on the other side of the walls would pay his pleadings no heed. Their guttural rumblings only confirmed this fact.

The kitchen butcher knife that Jerry managed to grab before the zombies crashed into his house could very well be his one and only chance at survival. Surely the flimsy, damp walls of a mere outdoor pole barn, one used to house is beloved 1972 Chevelle, would not keep them out. He thought how he should have never built his shed in the far corner of his yard. Then he would have fast access to useful and possibly deadly tools: steel rakes, grass clippers, shovels, even his axe, which he frequently used to chop up wood for both his fireplace in the house and his fire pit near the shed. Fond memories of sitting around a roaring bonfire roasting marshmallows and cooking hot dogs over the open flame slipped into his mind. He could practically taste a red-hot smore, its molten chocolate and gooey marshmallow oozing out the sides of the graham cracker.

God Almighty, what he'd give for a hot smore or a roasted hot dog right now. Or any other type of food for that matter. The faint, delectable aroma from an earlier, more pleasant, more normal time teased his senses with its flavor. But unfortunately for him, and possibly the rest of the world, he feared it was never to be again.

The zombies continued their assault on the pole barn. Scores of decayed hands clawed relentlessly on the three- quarter inch plywood sheets which made up the walls to the structure. Maroon paint flaked off the barn with each and every hit, mingling with the slate- gray flesh peelings from the zombie's bodies. Rows of bright yellow tulips were trampled beneath dead feet. Freshly seeded sod was mashed to a greenish muck. In-ground sprinkler heads, custom made by Jerry to hit all of the appropriate angles and corners, were crushed into plastic refuse by torn, shredded tennis shoes and filthy cowboy boots, by three-inch high heel pumps, by a pair of pink ballerina slippers, size one, which had become so stained with dried blood and other body fluids that they hardly resembled pink at all. Black was closer to their color now; the frilly, pink bows and ribbons on the tips of the shoes had been ripped off.

A tear welled up in Jerry's eye and slid down his cheek. Despite the dire situation he found himself in he still had trouble controlling his emotions. He clearly remembered buying those pink ballerina slippers. His little girl Wendy had worked on him for weeks to let her join the Highland Hills Dance Class in town. The cost was a bit steep, so Jerry had hesitated with making a decision, but he eventually gave in; nothing was too good for his little girl.

He recalled the dance place was a small building, only about three thousand square feet, but the rows and rows of various-sized trophies and plaques adorning the walls attested to its status and accomplishments in the field.

"Daddy pleeeese! I wanna dance. I wanna be a great dancer, the best in the whole world. Pleeeease!"

His little girl's words rung in his head as if she were standing in front of him saying them at that very moment. She was so happy when he finally gave in and signed her up for the class. She bragged to all of her friends, called her grandparents, and even wrote a letter to her imaginary friend Fanny. She said Fanny was so happy for her. Wendy's happiness meant everything to Jerry, and he vowed to always make sure she would stay that way.

His little girl's happiness…what a notion, one that he would never be able to enjoy, to experience ever again. For although he didn't know who exactly everyone was on the other side of the plywood walls of his pole barn, he did know with painful certainty who one of them was.

Wendy slammed her tiny, pallid fists into the barn, repeatedly, over and over again, constantly scraping bits and pieces of softened flesh from her hands and arms. Pale, blackish blood spurted from the cuts and oozed from the scrapes. But the little girl was oblivious to the injuries.

"Daddy?" she teased in a tone reminiscent of a sewer rat squealing in delight at finding some fresh carrion. "Daddy, you really need to take me to dance class now. Ms. Teamont told me not to be late. She said she doesn't like students who don't know how to tell time. She said I could be a really great dancer someday too. I show a lot of promise and could even be a professional one day if I work hard at it and really want it. Daddy? Daddy? Are you still in there?"

A sudden flash of recollection popped into Jerry's mind. Ms. Teamont, all ninety pounds of her, her coal-black hair pulled back into a bun so tightly that it looked painful, looming over the children in her dance class like an over-bearing parent. Her thin lips clamped together, leaving not the slightest trace of a mouth. Her piercing brown eyes burning holes into the very souls of the kids, not to mention the parents. Yes, Ms. Teamont in all of her domineering, strict glory.

"Oh Daddy, are you still there?" Wendy giggled through a smashed, bruised mouth and shattered baby teeth. "I know you still are. We all do. Every single one of us."

CHAPTER 2

The sun hung low in the crisp morning sky, veiled lightly by thin ribbons of wispy, vague clouds. The horizon was just below the sun, silhouetted in an attractive mixture of deep purple and reddish-orange, a faint reminder of the previous day and a promise of the upcoming one.

Jerry's eyes popped open. Immediately his head reminded him of the pressure, a dull throbbing pain only matched by the worst hangovers or bad head trauma. And it hurt even worse when the seething memories of what had happened the night before slid into his mind.

Had it been a dream? Some demented and frightening visions conjured up by his overactive imagination and possibly his love of junk food? Perhaps. And although he clung with all his remaining strength to the possibility that it had been a dream, he still couldn't deny the chance that it hadn't been one. The fact that he now found himself lying on the cold hard floor of his pole barn early in the morning with a throbbing head, a body that was wracked by stiffness and pain, and a memory stained by the haunting and quite possibly all-too-real occurrences of the previous night, attested to a very frightening scenario.

Rubbing his swollen eyes, Jerry gently lifted himself up. His rear end felt like it had been hit with a sledgehammer. He was terrified of what might still be lurking outside the barn, but realizing that he couldn't stay there forever, forced himself to stand. Eventually he would need food and water, and possibly even medical attention as well. Eventually he would need to know. Eventually. Inevitably.

His eyes glanced over at his prized 1972 pearl blue Chevelle. The early 70's General Motors mid-sized, two-door sedan sat underneath a dusty, beige tarp. The sleek outline of the car was mostly concealed by the car cover, but still offered its pleasant memories of happier times, albeit ones which usually required countless hours of skinned knuckles and greasy, uncomfortable, grime-coated overalls. Not to mention heated discussions with his wife Stephanie over the rising cost of maintaining and fixing up such a classic vehicle.

Stephanie, his lovely wife of nearly twenty years. God how he missed her. She had always nagged him to death, and her obsessive compulsion to keep things clean and organized drove him crazy, but he still loved her. He always had, from the very first moment he saw her; her soft eyes reflected a caring and passionate heart.

Jerry bit his lip to keep from crying when he remembered the happier times they'd shared: the birth of their children, saying their wedding vows before a packed church twenty years earlier, buying their first house together. There were really too many to count, too many pit stops in the long and unpredictable journey that was their life together.

The sharp, painful memory of the last time Jerry had seen his wife stabbed his heart with searing accuracy. It had been the previous night when this whole nightmare had apparently begun. He'd rolled over in bed, 3:07 a.m. staring at him in red, block numbers on the alarm clock. The day's previous events nudged him from a comfortable slumber into the dark and quiet confines of his bedroom. Mr. Tompsett, his overweight, overbearing, over-the-top supervisor at his dead end, but much needed job, had instructed Jerry in his usual crass way that he wanted the Bearings Proposal on his desk first thing in the morning on the following day. No excuses, no problems, nothing but the proposal signed, sealed, and delivered with all the t's crossed and the i's dotted. This unreasonable, and most likely unattainable deadline had fastened itself on Jerry's mind like a vulture on a fresh carcass. He had stayed late at the office that day and even worked through his lunch, stuffing a few vending machine snacks and a leftover turkey on rye into his mouth. And as five o'clock approached and slid into six o'clock and finally seven o'clock, he conceded to the fact that he would be forced to take the paperwork home with him. Stephanie would not like it, but he had no choice. Mr. Tempest had made sure of that.

Despite her deep sleep, Stephanie had sensed her husband's restlessness. She leaned up in bed and propped herself on an elbow. Jerry could see her outline in the dark and felt bad for having awakened her.

"What's the matter, Honey?" she asked groggily. "Can't you sleep?"

Jerry stretched a bit, pulling out a couple of pops from his neck and back. He looked over at Stephanie. Even in the darkness of the bedroom, he could still see the shapely silhouette of her body, her white and pink silk nightgown draped over her, her hair tangled from sleep.

"I can't sleep. I've just got too much on my mind. That jerk Tompsett wants the Bearings Proposal on his desk A.S.A.P. He knows perfectly well I can't meet that kind of deadline. I still have to crunch the numbers, and fax the copies to the right departments, and ..." He stopped himself in mid-sentence. He realized how he was running on and on to his poor wife who had her good night sleep interrupted by her stressed out husband. "I'm sorry, Steph. I didn't mean to babble on like that." Stephanie smiled at him. "It's all right, Honey," she replied quietly. "I think that's why our marriage has always been so strong. We listen to each other. Now just try to relax and in the morning I'll help you get your stuff together. I don't have to go into the office until noon. I'm only filling in for Sandy, and after I get Wendy off to school, I can give you a hand with your paperwork a little if you want."

Jerry smiled back at her. He had never loved her as much as at that moment. Even after twenty years of marriage, three kids, two mortgages, and a small bout with a frightening prostate issue, Stephanie had always stayed by his side. Always.

"I love you," Jerry whispered through the darkness.

"I love you too."

Then they shared a brief kiss and both promptly dozed back off.

I love you. What fitting last words he and Stephanie had said to each other on that fateful night.

When Jerry had looked at the alarm clock again, it read 5:22. For a brief, sleep-induced moment he almost thought it was the afternoon, but the tiny red dot next to the A.M. designation dispelled the notion. Stephanie was right next to him, her head facing the opposite direction, her face obscured by her long, brown hair and her pillow. Even before Jerry detected the smell, he knew something was wrong. He felt it in his bones, in his soul, in his heart.

Softly calling her name, he waited impatiently for a response that he knew deep down inside would never come.

"Steph? Honey, are you all right?" No answer. Only the silence, which filled the room, was present. And it revealed nothing.

"Stephanie, please answer me. Oh God, please answer me!"

Panic started to slip its noose around his mind at that moment. He knew she was dead. In fact, it suddenly occurred to him, her death throes were probably what had woken him up in the first place.

He didn't want to, but he reached over to the still form of his wife and felt her wrist. The absence of a pulse did not surprise him, but hurt just the same. She had died in her sleep, in their bed, right next to him. Most likely a heart attack; she always did have a weak heart. Her doctor had said it was nothing that a solid diet and steady exercise couldn't handle though. Apparently he was wrong.

Jerry's frenzied mind raced with panicked, incoherent thoughts, all jumbled together into a collection of vague importance. How long had she been dead? What was the last thing she thought of? Did she feel any pain? Was she looking down on him from Heaven?

Forcing himself to calm down, he leaned over her cold body and planted a soft kiss on her forehead, fighting the natural urges to recoil back. It was still his wife, his love, his Stephanie.

After he had covered the body with their blanket, he stumbled out of the room and down the hallway. Along the way he passed by Wendy and Seth's bedrooms. Both kids appeared to be sleeping peacefully. Pale moonlight from a horned moon filtered in through the windows, illuminating the still forms on their beds. All was quiet.

Just how he would break the news to his children that their mother was dead he did not know, but eventually he knew he would have to tell them. The fact that he was now a single father, a widower, was not lost on him, and only added to his crippling grief.

Jerry continued his trek down the hallway, ignoring the fact that he should call the authorities. He planned to, only not just yet. First he had to collect his thoughts and muster up whatever strength he could. After that he would wake the kids and inform them of the terrible news.

His oldest (Martin) was away at school at Kendell University in Akron, near the Michigan-Ohio border. He would be crushed when Jerry told him, and take the next flight home. Jerry needed him to be strong for the sake of Wendy and Seth, not to mention himself. Martin was a strong-willed type of young man, intelligent and resourceful, and his father had always admired those aspects of his personality, aspects that would now be tested to their fullest abilities.

A sad laugh escaped Jerry lips before he could stop it. The irony of the fact that he and Steph had constantly nagged Martin to visit home more often was a painful, bad joke. They would now get their wish: Martin would come home, but not for the reasons Jerry wanted.

A searing bolt of fear shot through Jerry's heart when he recalled those ominous words that followed him down that hallway that night.

"Oh, Dad. You woke us up. You made too much noise and woke us up."

Jerry whirled around, his face flush with tears and confusion. There standing in their respective doorways were his two youngest children. They were both chalk white and their faces reflected no signs of life. Their eyes were merely hollow orbs fastened in their heads, watching but seeing nothing, glossy windows to empty souls.

Wendy, Jerry's little girl, his pretty little princess, glared at him from her doorway. A thin, glistening trickle of bloody drool leaked from both corners of her tiny mouth, the same mouth that used to tell him that she loved him and that he was the best dad in the whole wide world, or used to complain when she had to brush her teeth, or do her homework, or clean her room.

"Oh, Daddy," Wendy slurred. "I really don't want to clean my room. It's not really that messy…except of course for Buffy's body."

Buffy was their dog. He was a cute, light brown terrier-poodle mix-breed which Jerry had rescued from a vacant lot one autumn day three years earlier. He had grown very much attached to that dog over the years, even going so far as to make her a doghouse with an adjoining room and built-in water and food bowls. He was proud of that doghouse having spent the better part of two months building it.

A fresh dose of agony ripped through Jerry's heart. First his wife, then two of his children, now his dog. The stress was becoming too much to bear. He fell backwards, banging into the wall behind him, knocking over a picture of the family taken on their recent trip to Mackinac Island. The frame of the smiling people in the photo crashed to the floor and shattered into an unrecognizable mess.

Jerry shuddered to think about what his poor little Buffy looked like or what she went through at the hands of the person whom she loved and trusted. Judging by the twisted expression on Wendy's face, it couldn't be very good.

Wendy and Seth stared hard at their father. Wendy's normally smooth complexion, which she went to great lengths to protect and nourish, was now darkening from the beginning stages of decomposition. Without her heart pumping the blood, her body was giving in to the effects of gravity; it was settling into the lower parts of her body as she stood.

Seth strolled up behind his dead sister and let a wicked smile slide across his pale face. "Hello, Dad," he stated in a no-nonsense tone.

Jerry began to back away from his kids, feebly reaching for something to arm himself with, although he knew in his weary heart that he would probably die before he could raise a hand to them.

Wendy and Seth's hands clenched in excitement and their soulless eyes widened, leaking greenish discharge. Wendy's head tilted to one side, releasing a series of sickening cracks and pops as her spine, deprived of a constant flow of healthy, circulating blood, started to dry up.

And then the two children lunged for their father.

CHAPTER 3

Sam Barrett stretched out his right arm while holding the cast iron exhaust manifold in place with his left. It was difficult to do, but over his many years, even decades, of working in the automotive trenches, he had developed certain skills, including ambidextrous ones. It was these unusual and often useful abilities which had enabled him to secure somewhat steady work throughout his life.

Sam had been at Old Man Feeter's Automotive Repair Haven for the better part of three years, most of them while living in Toals Creek, a textbook mid-western city, more ghost town than populated. He'd moved there after what he called *The Final Judgment* with his father. That decisive battle, a heated disagreement which rapidly escalated into an all out screaming match bordering on a brawl, literally forced Sam to finally pack his bags and move out of his father's house. He left behind memories, most of them bad, but faced his forced future with determination. He was good with cars and would eventually find work and take care of himself.

And so he crammed his belongings (toolboxes and some worn, second-hand clothes) into his 1977 red Chevy Malibu, never looking back.

Old Man Feeter's steel-toed work boots suddenly appeared behind Sam's head, the left one tapping impatiently on the oil-slicked floor of the shop.

"That you under there, Barrett?" Feeter's high-pitched voice squeaked. For such a large man, Feeter's high-pitched voice didn't match his body. Sam had always found that odd.

Sam winced in disgust as a fine, nearly invisible shower of cigar ashes drifted down from above him, eventually settling on and around the steel-toed boots. He struggled to maintain his grip on the exhaust manifold. He'd spent nearly twenty minutes simply trying to get the holes for the bolts lined up on the engine block and the last thing he wanted was to have to start over again. The flange on the manifold left very little room for error, only separating the bolt holes from the metal exhaust tubing about a quarter of an inch on all sides.

Sam suppressed his irritation. After all, Feeter was his boss.

"Yes sir, Mr. Feeter," he replied through gritted teeth. "I'm trying to finish the exhaust work on Mrs. Ether's Ford. She wants to pick it up by the end of the day. I told her I'd have it ready for her by then."

Sam heard his boss grumbling under his breath. The steel-toed work boot continued its incessant tapping, almost rhythmically, as more pungent cigar ashes drifted down to the floor.

"Very well then, Barrett," Feeter finally snorted, his voice full of annoyance. "Just make it snappy, will ya? I've got plans in life, big plans, and keeping customers waiting, keeping their money waiting, is not in my agenda. Do I make myself clear?"

Sam bit down on his lip hard. It was all he could do to keep from telling Feeter off.

"Yes, sir," he replied as calmly as he could. "I understand completely."

The steel-toed work boots turned and slowly walked away, leaving the strong odor of cigar smoke behind.

"Jerk," Sam whispered under his breath. "If I didn't need this crappy job so much, I'd…I'd…"

You'd what? the voice asked sarcastically. *You don't have the guts to do anything about it, do you? Well, do you?*

Sam winced in pain. His arm was growing numb from holding the exhaust manifold in place for so long.

"Get lost," he grunted. "I don't need any crap from you. I got enough to deal with every day already. Just leave me alone."

Of course you do. But you still haven't the guts to tell Old Man Feeter off, do you? You wimp. You can't even tell him how much easier your crummy job would be if he would just peel open his enormous bank account and install a hydraulic lift in this place. You wouldn't have to lie on your back like a bum anymore. You could get to hard-to-reach parts much easier. You'd double your productivity, and then maybe, just maybe, you could stop talking to yourself so much.

Sam fought back the tears again. They were like a dam, his

worries about how others perceived his behavior, the cement wall holding back the immense, relentless weight and pressure of the water. But inevitably, as so many times in the past, the wall would crumble, releasing a gushing torrent of pent-up frustrations.

Gripping the exhaust manifold as tight as his aching arm would allow, Sam pressed the metal tubing against the engine block. With his free hand he scrambled for the bolts, and locating three of them right away, began the laborious ask of fastening them to the manifold, securing the part snugly in place. Relief washed over him when he was finally able to release the manifold from his grasp. The burn in his arms subsided immediately.

The sharp noise stung Sam's ears and rattled his thoughts. It sounded as if someone had fallen over, somebody in Feeter's office. Sam set down his open-end wrench and carefully slid himself out from under Mrs. Ether's Ford. It had been many days since he last took his medication and he felt his head start to grow light as he stood up. The room began to take on a foggy, blurred type of look, a faintly greenish mist cascading down from seemingly impossible sources. A small radio, amidst the usual cluster one might find in an auto repair shop, began to sputter, slicing out bits and pieces of music and lyrics before abruptly choking off the song altogether.

Sam's heart was in his throat. His head spun around the room. His body felt cold; steel shivers were shooting down his spine. He began to wonder if it was all due to his failure to take his pills. The doctor had told his father about the laundry list of problems that could happen if he were to forget his medication, and Sam remembered clearly that some of them were disorientation, headaches, and hallucinations. Hallucinations. Maybe that's what was plaguing him. Just his mind playing tricks on him.

A similar noise to the one before startled him again from his thoughts. It was very much like the first sound, only more pronounced in its severity and its volume.

Feeling the all-too real possibility that what was happening was not a hallucination, Sam realized that he must find something with which to defend himself.

Miss July stared down at him from a nearby wall, her trim body scantily- clad in a thin, bright yellow bathing suit. Directly beneath the provocative calendar was a scattered selection of various wrenches, sockets, and screwdrivers. Sam moved over toward the workbench, trying his best to remain quiet. His head still ached and he still felt cold but he ignored it.

Whatever had made the noises was definitely coming from Feeter's office. Sam grasped a large, partially rusted crescent wrench from the workbench and tested its weight. It swung heavy in his hand, proving it to be a worthy makeshift weapon.

Feeter's office window was off to his right, nestled snugly between towering stacks of tires, tool cabinets, and hanging rows of various-sized fan belts and air cleaners. A strange thought flashed in Sam's mind: *Did they have the right- sized fan belt for Mrs. Ether's car?*

Sam gripped the wrench tightly in his sweaty hand, and took a few tentative steps toward the window. He wanted to see if Feeter was in his office, but hoped against all hope that he wasn't. The room continued to sway. The mist continued to float about. The dream, the hallucinations that Sam hoped it all was, continued. His head still ached; he still felt cold.

Feeter's window came closer and closer as Sam worked his way through the room. He leaned forward, straining to see if anyone was there, but a frost had developed on the glass, partially obscuring the office behind it, hiding who, or what might be lurking within it. Overhead, the dingy florescent light fixtures dangled from rusty, leftover wire that Sam himself had rigged up. The light emanating from them was sparse at best, periodically flickering like seen in so many horror movies.

Sam took a second or two to ponder the unique and frightening situation he found himself in: the faint, greenish mist, the strange noises coming from Mr. Feeter's office, the frost on the office window, the radio sputtering out for no good reason, and finally the flickering lights. Surely if all these strange occurrences were only hallucinations, he would know it somehow. Even hallucinations had many holes, breaks in the veil of reality that they wore that could usually be detected.

Sam approached the window cautiously with the wrench held out in front of him. Instinctively he started to crouch down, just to be on the safe side, but eventually he knew he would have to look into Feeter's office. Raising himself up slowly, he peered past the glass.

The torn, gore-streaked face of Old Man Feeter sneered back at him, strands of bloody tissue dangling loosely from his grinning mouth.

CHAPTER 4

The rusty nail head invaded the soft flesh of Ryan's arm as he pivoted around to exit the dark, dusty confines of the attic. Sticky, feather-light cobwebs from long dead spiders silently cascaded down from above and coated his hair and shoulders. The numerous boxes and various discarded possessions from the home's previous owners littered nearly every square inch of the space, and it was nothing short of a small miracle that Ryan had managed to infiltrate the attic at all, much less explore the long-forgotten containers and debris strewn about every which way.

He looked at his forearm where he had been stabbed by the nail. A small pool of blood welled up in the tiny puncture wound, further heightening his annoyance at his own carelessness. He hated the sight of blood, most of all his own. He always had, ever since he was a little kid and he skidded off his bike, scraping his knees along the pitted, course surface of the concrete. The sight of the crimson sheen slicked across his legs sent him into a frenzied panic. And when the wound's unwelcome companion (pain) came around, he really freaked out.

Blood and pain. The two always seemed to be inexorably linked together, a frightful pair lurking near every potential accident site.

Ryan pulled an old handkerchief from his pocket and wrapped it around the puncture wound. It wasn't much, but would be somewhat adequate protection from further loss of blood or possible infection. Pride of accomplishment filled his head and spawned far-fetched images of vast fortunes and worldwide fame. He knew very well his imagination was running away with him, but entertained the notion of the rewards regardless. He would be able to quit his job at the machine shop and travel the world, possibly in first class. The unique items he had uncovered in the attic just had to be worth something; he could feel it in his bones.

Clutching the antiques tightly to his chest, Ryan began to crawl toward the access opening to the attic. His arm was starting to throb (he must have jabbed it pretty deeply), but he ignored it. As long as he made it out of the attic in one piece; he could wash the wound and apply some antiseptic when he got to the bathroom.

A tiny drop of blood dripped from the nail tip and fell onto the attic floor behind him, forming a dime-sized circle of red on the old, useless insulation that lay between the joists.

Ryan didn't notice. He concentrated on reaching the access opening. Getting back to the real world with his possessions was all that mattered to him now; that and listing them on eBay.

*   *   *

The tattered remains of what used to be Wade Boulter, Ryan's next door neighbor and frequent suburban adversary, stopped in its grisly feast. It suddenly flashed its mottled head from side to side, successfully tearing off a thick chunk of dripping innards from its pet dog. The canine visceral dangled grotesquely from its glistening mouth.

It had heard something. Something nearby. Something very nearby, apparently coming from its neighbor's house... Ryan's house. And it had also smelled something. It smelled blood. Freshly fallen from a fresh wound, still warm. It was like a lighthouse beacon on a foggy, rain-swept night moving across the swirling waters of the sea. The drop of blood called to Wade Boulter's corpse, and it intended to answer that call by whatever means necessary.

Wade hesitated for a moment and then stumbled to his feet, temporarily balancing himself against a small coffee table. Past issues of *Modern Drummer Magazine* fell to the stained carpet. He had been thumbing through several of them when the chest pains started and extinguished his life in an instant, a fitting but unfortunate end.

Reading them had been a source of interest for Wade when he was alive. The noise from his Starcaster Tama drum set when he rifled through the many chops he had developed over the years always drove his wife and kids crazy. He had developed his own unique style, utilizing a cross of precision technique and smooth, almost improvisational approach which borrowed heavily on the standard twenty-six basic drum rudiments. Normally the two wouldn't really mesh together that well, they seemed to contradict one another, but he made them work.

Wade smiled to himself. He bent down and snatched the May 2002 issue up in his gray, bloated hand. Finger joints, stiffened by rigor mortis and decay, cracked like an ice cube in a steaming cup of tea. Dead, clouded eyes gazed down in stupid wonderment at the magazine cover.

DREAM THEATER'S MIKE PORTNOY was splattered across the front of the issue, with the progressive drumming great's large picture underneath the heading. Portnoy was grinning from ear to ear while holding a pair of his signature nylon-tipped drumsticks across his chest; his massive, multi-tiered drum set complete with nearly a dozen brass cymbals was positioned behind him as if anticipating its owner's arrival.

WIN A COMPLETE PEARL MASTER'S CUSTOM MMX 7-PIECE DRUM SET! was directly beneath the title of the magazine in bold, red lettering.

And: *ADVANCE YOUR MUSICAL CAREER! EDUCATIONAL OPPORTUNITIES FOR 2002 AND BEYOND*! It was circled in black permanent marker on the left hand side of the issue.

The last section of the cover caught Wade's eye as a faint memory of his former life drifted into his decaying mind. He remembered how he had wanted to pursue a musical career, so much so that he had circled the article to remind himself to look into it. He was planning on researching the possibilities and eventually presenting his ideas to Sally and the kids when he got the chance. He knew deep down inside that it wasn't exactly a responsible career path to follow, but his heart was in it, and when he was behind his drum set, nothing else mattered to him. It was his dream, his passion, and hopefully, his destiny.

But then on this one day, he dropped dead of a massive heart attack, fittingly enough, while he was playing his drums. There had been no warning, no alarm bells, nothing whatsoever to indicate that he, a seemingly healthy, active, intelligent man of forty-one, was about to run out of gas.

Too bad God didn't equip humans with a fuel gauge.

He was simply seated comfortably behind his kit one minute, happily practicing his press rolls and double bass chops, and the next minute he was lying with his frozen face mashed against one of his bass drum pedals, the felt tip wedged tightly against his rapidly cooling forehead.

In a brief lapse of distorted time and space he wondered if he was going to be heading for that final light at the end of the tunnel. Only there wasn't any light. And no tunnel. And nothing final about the whole experience at all.

And then he found himself alive again, and yet not alive. His head and back felt stiff, his limbs rigid and sore, his mind aware, but clotted with a strange host of new priorities. His wife and children, his house, his job, his golf clubs, his fishing pole, his drum set, even his own health and well-being were no longer on his list of what was important. All that mattered to him now was finding food, and not for nourishment, or even enjoyment. He wanted food only to assuage the gnawing and irresistible urges which were overcoming him. Only to quiet the terrible pain that wracked his mind. Only to give in to the inevitable and experience the overwhelming euphoria that most certainly awaited him.

Wade felt like crying. He wanted to unhinge the floodgates and let the waters flow unhindered. He wanted to release all the pent up rage and grief. But no tears came. His eyes were merely rotating balls of rapidly drying out tissue. Organs which served no purpose anymore. There was no soul left behind those eyes. It simply was not there.

Wade dropped the magazine into the clutter on the floor, and reaching up, plucked one of his eyeballs from its socket. The Optic Nerve dangled from the hole, writhing slightly as if it were attempting to locate the remainder of the organ.

He studied it with his remaining eye, marveling at how it functioned, and then, quickly losing interest, tossed it aside. It plopped onto the floor on the other side of the room, a near-translucent red smear all around it.

The strange new urges Wade felt were impeding all other thoughts in his head. Sally, the kids, his long-dead dream of playing his drums professionally, all were being smothered, devoured by some powerful, unknown force that he knew was somehow behind his re-animation.

He stumbled out of his living room, bouncing off a recliner, a coffee table, an ottoman. Numerous items in the room crashed to the floor. Leftover plates of food tipped over and scattered onto the carpet, leaving unrecognizable piles. Lamps tumbled off of end tables, shattering on impact with dust-coated hardwood floors. Pictures fell from walls, coming apart as they collided with the ground, years of happier times captured on film destroyed in an instant.

Wade paid none of it any attention. He bent down and slid a large, jagged piece of glass out of his left foot, leaving a clean, thin slit from which blackish, thickening blood seeped. He felt neither pain from the wound, nor any loss of the motor functions in his body. When he was alive, his first concern over such a deep cut would have been it affecting his ability to play his drums up to his personal standards. But not now. Now the gash only roused what morbid curiosity he possessed.

The half-eaten remains of his dog lay on the white-tiled kitchen floor. A gaping hole was carved out of its midsection, and glistened with canine gore. Once- intricate organs and streaming blood vessels were now a mass of unmoving slop, slicked with rotted blood and scraps of partially chewed tissue.

Wade stumbled over to his deceased pet and gazed down at the bloody mess he had created. He felt no remorse, no sorrow, no feelings for his dog whatsoever. He used to love his dog, even taking him fishing with him down at Houghton Lake occasionally. But now he simply did not care anymore. The strange new urges were controlling his actions now.

The corpse of Wade Boulter stepped over the remains of its pet and walked into the kitchen. The dining table was still set with multi-colored bowls filled with stale, soggy Rice Krispies and spoiled Two-percent milk. Unused spoons poked out from the stagnant mixtures.

Wade glanced at the settings and then at the bodies of his wife and two children seated at the table. Sally, her long auburn hair stained with her blood, leaned back in her chair. The portion of her face that was still left sagged under the weight of her head. A look of disbelief was mixed with one of terror and pain. Wade could still detect in her clouded-over eyes the image of the last thing she had seen: her dead husband advancing on her and their two kids with teeth gnashing and blood dripping.

The children were seated similarly, each sporting their own fatal wounds and bite marks. The youngest one still clutched a cup half full of grape juice.

Wade turned away from his grisly, former meals and stepped toward the door. It led straight out into the backyard. His brand new Genesis EP-310 barbeque stood nearby, wearing memories of good family times. He walked past it before doubling back to stare at his pride and joy. A sliver of the past tried to squirm its way into his mind, attempting to recall the happiness that he'd felt when he brought the appliance home for the first time. The center-mounted thermostat stared at him like a single eye. Past thoughts of hamburgers and thick steaks sizzling on the grill drifted into the air. But he didn't care. He had no interest anymore in such things. There was plenty of fresh meat available anywhere he looked, including in his own home.

The sounds coming from his neighbor's house caught his attention. The noises were distinct and yet vague.

Wade started to walk through his backyard toward Ryan's house.

CHAPTER 5

Sam slowly backed away from the window. He struggled to maintain his grip on the wrench, not to mention his sanity. The fact that he was witnessing his boss, Mr. Feeter, as an obviously homicidal lunatic bumbling around in his office, strained Sam's courage to the point of breaking. He felt weak.

"Ahh, good. My best employee," Feeter drawled through mechanically gyrating teeth. "I've been wondering where you have been."

Sam watched in disgust as pulpy gristle dripped from Feeter's mouth, staining the front of his torn shirt. His stomach churned, his head throbbed, his knees threatened to buckle, and as much as he wanted to, he couldn't tear his eyes away from the grotesque spectacle. Was any of what was happening real? Zombie bosses, weird green mists; it was beginning to be too much for him to bear.

The thin pane of glass between them was no match for Feeter's driving hunger and clenched fists. It shattered with the first blow, sending dozens of jagged shards of glass crashing to the ground in a violent explosion. Feeter peered through the opening. Behind him, sprawled across the floor of his office, was the half-eaten body of Tim, his teenage son who had occasionally helped out at the shop with paperwork and errands. Sam had lunch with him only a few days earlier Tim complained to him how his dad never let him get his hands dirty. He wanted to work on the cars, to learn exactly how engines and drivetrains worked. But his father told him that that was work for grunts, people who weren't good enough to manage real work, or handle real problems, or deal with real money.

Sam tore his horrified gaze away from Tim's remains. A flash of guilt streaked across his conscience. He wanted to grieve for Tim; he was a good kid, honest and hardworking, but Sam had other things to worry about at the moment. Things like Mr. Feeter punching his way through the wall to get to him.

"I see you, Sam," Feeter snorted through all the commotion. "I just want to go over some repairs you made. The customers brought the cars back. They were really ticked off too. They said you did a lousy job. They want their money back."

Feeter was scowling as he continued smashing through the wall, oblivious to the flying debris. "I can't have that, you know," he said with a dark undertone. "I can't be giving customers back their money. It wouldn't be good for business, and as you know I have plans in life."

Sam cringed as Feeter's hand shot through the wall, drywall dust sticking to the putrefaction.

"There we go," Feeter mused. "Now we're getting somewhere."

His other hand punched through, followed immediately by his right foot. The wallboard crumbled from the assault. Glass crunched beneath his steel-toed work boots as the zombie finally stepped into the shop. A sly, uneven grin was plastered across its pallid face. It stood still as it sized up its prey.

"Look busy, Sam," it sneered through clenched, bloody teeth. "The boss is in!"

Sam jumped to his feet, his fear overcome by his instinct to survive. His overalls snagged a small vice perched on the edge of a nearby workbench. It tore a thin strip of fabric and flesh loose. Sam ignored it as Feeter advanced toward him.

The zombie's eyes were clouded, void of any emotion, any humanity. It moved closer and closer to Sam, but very slowly. Each crooked step induced a whole new level of fear in its prey, and it knew this, relishing it like a killer whale toying with a wounded seal.

The dangling piece of fabric that had ripped from Sam's clothes suddenly gave him an idea. He pulled off the strip with one quick yank. Next to the vice on the bench was a Holly 600 cfm carburetor. He was going to rebuild it when he got the chance and install it in his Malibu. It probably would have been too much for the camshaft to handle, but it would have been free; it was a leftover piece of equipment he rescued from an abandoned Chevy Nova behind the shop.

Gripping the carb tightly, he flipped it over, exposing the jet ports on its underside. He stuffed the fabric into one of the ports and jammed it down as far as it would go, being sure to leave a small piece hanging out the end. A jar of old gasoline, which he planned to use to prime the carb, sat off to the side, flanked by numerous tools and boxes. Sam sensed Feeter coming up behind him; he could hear chunks of his boss's body literally falling off of him and slithering to the floor. Rotted flesh sloughed down, forming a sickening soup of rot. Feeter either didn't notice or didn't care. Either way it was a terrible sight, worthy of any horror author's imagination.

Sam did his best to concentrate on his makeshift weapon. He didn't have much time before Feeter would be on him, but he felt it would be his best chance at killing the thing. He fumbled in his back pocket for his lighter. It had been a gift from an old friend of his when he was just a kid, and since he didn't smoke, it managed to stay in workable condition after all these years. But he came up empty-handed. Feeter was closing in on him, licking his blackened chops with a swollen, purple tongue.

You better hurry up there, son, his father's leering image urged from the wall next to Miss July and her yellow bikini. *Don't have too much time left, ya know.* The face glanced over at the swimsuit calendar. *See. Even she's turning against you.*

Sam watched open-mouthed as the provocative picture of Miss July, labeled as Jenny, began to squirm on the paper. The once-attractive features she displayed: long, flaxen hair swirling behind her head in the photo shoot's fans, the doe-eyed expression of innocence reminiscent of the girl next door who had just been caught with her hand in the cookie jar, the seductive pose, (hands on hips, back arched to one side, chest heaved forward), they all now seemed to be distorted somehow.

Sam rubbed his eyes and looked again.

Miss July, "Jenny" to her many male fans, was growing paler, mottled, almost as if she were becoming some sort of...zombie.

Fine green mist sprinkled down from an unknown source and speckled the calendar, further adding to the swimsuit model's raw, smeared beauty.

"You and your stupid posters," Feeter grunted. "You always were some type of weirdo."

Sam pulled his gaze away from the calendar. The Holly 600 carburetor still sat on the table in front of him. He had to finish it quickly before Feeter reached him.

You never were any good at finishing things, son, Sam's father chimed in. *You know it and I know it. That's one of the reasons we never got along too well. Are you listening to me, Boy?*

Sam pushed his father's face from his mind. He needed to concentrate. He could smell the stench of rotting flesh stronger with each step Feeter took. It was making his eyes water and his stomach churn. If he would have had anything in his belly, he surely would have thrown it up right then and there.

Sam! Listen to me boy! I'm talking to you!

Sam finally found his lighter (it was in his rear pocket, next to his wallet) and yanked it out immediately. He tipped the remaining fuel from the jar into the top choke opening on the carb, slid the flap shut tightly, and grabbed a loose spark plug wire from the floor. It had been in Mrs. Ether's Ford; Sam was doing a complete tune-up on her car after he finished with the exhaust.

He tied the wire around the body of the carb, leaving a length hanging so he could swing it like a slingshot. A flick of the lighter ignited the makeshift weapon, which quickly became engulfed with flames.

"What ya got there?" Feeter breathed down Sam's neck. He was standing directly behind him, his teeth grinding in anxious excitement.

Sam didn't reply. With one violent motion, he grabbed the wire, spun around, and whirled the flaming piece of metal straight into the side of Feeter's head. The force of the blow knocked the corpse sideways, its softening body crumbling to the oil-slicked floor of the shop.

Sam stood there, panting heavily as he tried to catch his breath. Streaks of blackened blood striped his face and arms. His clothes were wet with perspiration. His eyes were wide with the realization that he succeeded in stopping Mr. Feeter.

It's about time you did something right, his father added in a satisfactory tone. *But I'm still not that proud of you, Boy. You could've just killed that boss of yours with some of those old tools you have all around here.*

"Shut up!" Sam suddenly screamed. "I'm sick of you and all your crap! You hear me! I'm sick of it! I needed to use some creativity. Some ingenuity. Don't you understand that? I had to be creative about it!"

Sam looked down at the smoldering corpse at his feet. It hardly resembled the man who had done him the favor of hiring him when he so desperately needed a job. But Feeter was also verbally abusive and pushed Sam to the limit countless times with his unrealistic demands. He often wondered just how Feeter's son Tim managed to keep his cool with a father like that.

Before he could stop himself, Sam released all of the bottled up rage and frustration inside and unleashed a savage kick to Feeter's torso. His foot sunk into the smoking flesh like it was warm butter. Disgusted, Sam immediately pulled his foot back out, shaking it to remove as much of the gore as he could. His boot dripped with the mess.

And then he turned around, intent on walking out of Feeter's Automotive Repair Haven for the last time. He wasn't going to look back, not even once. He was going to turn the page in the book of his life. New chapters awaited him, for better or worse, and he was planning on delving into each and every one headfirst. He would have to find another job, but after what he'd just been through that would be the least of his worries.

Miss July glared at him from her perch on the wall. The strange green mist continued to sprinkle down from nowhere in particular, and his father's face silently watched him walk past.

"Goodbye, Dad," Sam muttered without really meaning it. "I know Mom wouldn't like it, but I doubt I'll ever see you again."

And then Sam found himself lying on the floor of the shop. The back of his head throbbed where it had smacked into the concrete.

Greasy, thin trickles of his blood mixed with the oil and grime in the room.

"What the…" he mumbled. He was surprised that nobody responded to his words. "What happened?"

The monotonous ticking of the clock on the wall echoed in the shop. Its steady ticks were in rhythm with the pounding in Sam's head. He sat up, instinctively rubbing his temples. The rigged-up fluorescent light fixtures hummed softly from above, directly into his eyes, and he cursed under his breath at them.

When he looked at the palm of his hand, it was smeared with red.

"Great. Just great. A head wound."

However, all around him seemed normal. Miss July was looking as sexy as ever. Mrs. Ether's Ford was propped up on one side, its exhaust system partially dismantled. The Holly 600 carburetor from the old Nova behind the building lay on the workbench, a smudged jar of stale gasoline sitting next to it.

And Mr. Feeter's body, his smashed, rotting body was thankfully nowhere to be found.

Sam finally concluded that it must have been hallucinations after all, and vowed to himself to start taking his medication again. He ran his fingers through his hair and straightened his clothes.

"Yeah, that's what it must have been. Hallucinations. Just my imagination running away with me."

The ragged corpse of Mr. Feeter momentarily stopped in its grisly feast. The torn body of its son Tim was outstretched before it, a sagging pile of entrails. He had heard another voice in the shop. Looking up, his face coated in a shiny, crimson sheen, Feeter stumbled to his feet and headed toward the office window.

CHAPTER 6

It took a while but Jerry finally managed to open the door to the pole barn. He gave a passing thought to the notion of hot-wiring his Chevelle and simply barreling out of the barn full bore. It would be a brave testament to mankind's desire to survive and persevere. Of man's superior intellect and ability to adapt to a changing world, even one where the dead stood. But he dismissed the idea. He hated to admit it, but it would have been painful to put his beloved classic muscle car through the ringer like that. After all the money, and blood, and sweat, and tears he'd poured into it, he just couldn't do it. And he also didn't relish the idea of all the commotion it would cause either. Stealth was a far more preferable alternative, at least until he knew exactly what he was up against.

The rod on the slide-bolt lock Jerry installed only a few weeks before made a light squeak as he slid it over. He winced in fear, his breath catching in his throat.

"One down, two to go," he whispered to himself. "I can do this. I can. Just got to be *Double Q* that's all. *Double Q* is all I need."

Double Q, as he dubbed it, stood for Quick and Quiet, just the two attributes he needed to successfully employ if he hoped to stay alive.

But what was there to stay alive for? His wife was dead. At the very least, two of his three children were dead. And they weren't only dead. They were undead. They were damn zombies for Pete's sake! And furthermore, for all he knew he might just be the last one in town still alive. Or the last one in Michigan. Or the last one in the country. Or the last one on the planet! And the chilling thought was made all the more frightening by the fact that it could quite possibly be true, or at least partially true.

Removing his sweaty hand from the slide bolt, Jerry reluctantly reached down to the chain lock. Likening it to removing a band-aid, he swiftly moved the chain off its bracket in one quick move. He grimaced at the noise it made.

"One more," he whispered to no one. "Just one more. Then

we'll see what's waiting for me."

Painful memories tried to push their way into his head: Wendy and Seth's faces when they confronted him in the dark hallway, Stephanie's cold body in the bed next to him on that fateful night, the fact that everything he loved in life could very well be completely drained of its importance and significance. Nothing mattered anymore. Fishing trips to Alcov Lake, watching the ball game at Teddy's Tavern with the guys, the science fiction mystery novel he was getting ready to begin working on. None of it meant anything anymore.

A single tear welled in his eye and rolled down his cheek, pooling on his upper lip. He fought back the urge to burst out crying; the loss of his wife and two of his children was almost too much for him to bear. But there were two things that kept him going: The hope that his oldest son, Martin, was alive and uninfected, and his will to live. He wanted to live and he vowed to himself that he would never give up, even if it meant sacrificing everything he held so dear, including his own sanity. He would go down fighting, fighting for not only his own life, but for the lives of any other still-breathing human being. And somehow, some way he would get to Martin.

With these thoughts giving him some much needed courage Jerry reached down to release the third and final lock on the door.

The breeze was picking up slightly from the north, bringing with it a cool stench of chilled rot, similar to rancid meat. Jerry noticed this unpleasant and alarming aroma in the air. He realized right away that he hadn't been dreaming and this caused a thick lump to form in his throat. Again he turned and looked at his beloved muscle car hidden beneath its dusty car cover. He entertained the notion of trying to get it started over and over again, but in the end decided against it. At least not yet.

The brass doorknob felt cold in his hand. Very cold. But he hardly noticed. He'd heard nothing on the other side of the door except for the wind whistling through the trees. It was safe; it had to be.

Snatching a pipe wrench from his toolbox, Jerry readied the tool in front of him like a weapon. He took a deep breath and twisted the doorknob, releasing the lock mechanism. The door creaked open, revealing the stillness outside. A few early morning sparrows soared by overhead. Trees and bushes swayed with the breeze. And the odor of rot clung to everything.

Jerry nervously peeked out of the crack. A thin line of early morning daylight was all he saw at first, but his eyes adjusted and noticed the rear door of his house, a dark rectangle that seemed a million miles away. It represented a pathway to safety, his home, or at the very least, comfortable, familiar surroundings that would allow him to gather his thoughts and some much needed supplies. His thirst was raging and his stomach was threatening to shut down, so he was not allowed the luxury of taking his time to make sure the coast was clear.

A twig snapped from behind a row of arborvitaes. "Wendy?" he blurted out before he could help himself; he quickly clasped his hand over his mouth. He had to use his wits. He knew perfectly well that his youngest wasn't alive anymore. And she wasn't dead either; she was something in between. For all he knew, those things, including his own kids, could still be lurking around outside just waiting for him to expose himself by leaving the safety of the pole barn.

The door squeaked a little more as Jerry nudged it open further. Fortunately everything outside seemed to be quiet. Thankful for small miracles, he made the sign of the cross over his chest, raised the pipe wrench up to his face, and slowly walked out into his yard.

He resisted the urge to bolt for his house right away, instead opting for a slow, more cautious approach; there was less chance of drawing attention to himself. His throat felt like sandpaper and a garden hose lay right next to the rear door of the house, but again, he decided to pass it up. Although he was badly dehydrated, turning on a hose bib might make too much noise.

The house projected a strange aura. It was his home still, the same place he'd spent so many hours and so much money fixing up. The same place he and Stephanie were going to grow old in together and play with their grandchildren in. But now the house felt like it didn't belong to him. The stillness owned it now, and possibly the zombies as well.

Taking baby steps, Jerry gradually inched his way along the

asphalt walkway toward the house. His eyes darted from side to side, back and forth, being ever aware, ever cautious of his surroundings and all the potential dangers it might conceal. He was relieved that the morning was quiet, almost peaceful. Only a few insects chirped or buzzed, and the wind had died down considerably.

The door stuck at first, causing Jerry to curse himself for not oiling it before. It was just one of the many items on the house that he meant to address but kept putting off for various reasons. With a bit of courage, he gave the door a light shove with his shoulder and quickly whirled around to make sure he was still alone.

The yard was empty.

The door swung open, revealing the laundry room to him. Instantly, the stench of death wafted into his face. Shadows were scattered everywhere; the morning had not yet penetrated the house. Jerry entered the room, which was adjacent to the kitchen. A single wall separated the two rooms with a small, windowless opening cut into it near the broom closet.

Jerry stepped through the room, pausing temporarily when he reached the washer and dryer. The fact that he probably would never have to do laundry ever again brought a smile to his face; it was the one job around the house he always hated doing. Stephanie usually did the clothes.

The fond memories washed over him like a tidal wave. He tried to suppress them as much as he could, but couldn't hold back the waters. In a rush of emotion, mingled with sheer exhaustion, the tears came.

"Is that you, Honey?" the familiar voice asked from the kitchen. It was literally dripping with dark sarcasm.

Jerry froze where he stood, frantically wiping away the tears from his face. He knew who the voice belonged to and how impossible it was he was hearing her. But then he remembered how the impossible had recently become possible, even commonplace.

It was his wife. It was Stephanie.

CHAPTER 7

Cliff pushed the stainless-steel cart down the dimly lit hallway. His stubbled face reflected not only the boredom of his day, but also his life. His job at Abby Convalescent Home was yet another dead end in a long string of broken promises and short-lived dreams. He had no girlfriend, his parents hardly knew he existed, and the only thing he was ever any good at (playing guitar) proved to be an express ticket to failure when he tried to pursue a musical career.

A tedious sigh slipped past his lips and echoed in the silence of the hallway. Just another day at work, like the day before and the day before that. He was responsible for delivering various commodities to the elderly folks who resided in the building: reading material, small portable games, and the occasional soda pop or healthy snack.

The cart rolled along the dull white floor tiles, which were so dirty they were
closer to a pale yellow. Cliff's head bounced from side to side.

"Carry on my wayward son. There'll be peace when you are done. Lay your weary head to rest. Dont'cha cry no more."

The classic rock opus reverberated in Cliff's ears, courtesy of the group Kansas. He temporarily lost himself in the catchy melody. He didn't notice the strange shadow up ahead. It sprayed itself on the wall across from Room C-3.

The stainless-steel cart stopped rolling. Cliff stared at the silhouette. It resembled an elderly man hunched over and gulping down chunks of something like a wild animal. Steve Walsh's distinct vocals were silenced with a click of the stop button on the Walkman.

"Hello?" Cliff called out tersely. A lump was forming in his throat, making it difficult to swallow. "W…who's there?"

The shadow stopped for a moment, looked up in his direction, and then continued with its strange feast. A soft grunting sound accompanied the figure's movements.

Cliff's inner voice, the one that looked out for him when he was a little boy, the one that kept him from making bad decisions or saying foolish things, warned him to back off. But his adventurous side, the one that wanted him to explore his world, to seek out new experiences and discover new ways of looking at things, said otherwise. It reasoned that nothing else in his bland life could compare to something like this, and although it could be dangerous, he would never be able to forgive himself if he passed the opportunity up. In short, he had nothing to lose.

Except perhaps his life.

Gripping his pocketknife tightly, Cliff advanced slowly toward the shadow. He decided not to call out to it again, adopting surprise as his best weapon. As he approached the doorway, he felt his courage slipping away. But he knew he couldn't turn back, mainly due to the shadow apparently sensing him coming. It ceased devouring its grisly meal and turned its malformed head in his direction, growling like a rabid dog. In one swift motion Cliff stepped into the doorway and gazed in stupid amazement at what was casting the shadow.

"May I help you, young man?" the aged man asked through a toothless smirk. His glassy eyes squinted with glazed-over annoyance as his dried out brow wrinkled from his facial expressions.

Cliff immediately retracted his small pocketknife, a persistent reluctance to do so gnawing at his mind.

"I…I'm sorry," he stammered, feeling somewhat embarrassed. "I didn't know you were…"

The old man snickered in disgust. "You punks always have to stick your noses where they don't belong. Can't you just leave me alone?"

Cliff forced a superficial smile and backed out of the room. He felt bad, but also irritated. The old guy didn't have to be so rude. He didn't mean to disturb him. Normally he wouldn't have given the incident another thought, but his memory kept replaying the disturbing shadow he'd seen, or thought he had seen, over and over again in his mind.

Did he imagine it?

Maybe, maybe not. But just to play it safe, he decided to avoid Room C-3 as much as he could.

*   *   *

Two days passed and Cliff had, for the most part, been successful in staying away from C-3 or any neighboring rooms. Only twice was he forced to pass by the room: the first time the door was thankfully closed, and the second time he didn't see any signs of the old man, although he did hear someone stirring in the bathroom.

The temptation to quit his job did enter Cliff's mind frequently. He would simply put in his notice, and then two weeks later (or sooner if he chose), he'd be free of Abby Convalescent Home forever. Or better yet he could just walk away. People did it all the time. He wouldn't be the first.

But inevitably, there were problems with his master plan. First off, just where would he go? His life seemed to have no real purpose, and at least now he had a job, a paycheck, and some security. And secondly, it still wouldn't solve the problem of what he saw in C-3. That, he feared, would be ingrained in his mind for the rest of his life, whether he imagined it or not.

Cliff sighed when the implications of quitting his job sunk in and the wild notion slipped away into the untouchable realm of impossibility. Just because he saw some old man in Room C-3 crouched over eating something didn't mean anything. With a grunt of resentment he finally decided he'd keep his dead end job, even if it meant having to eventually face whatever was in C-3. He wasn't too proud to admit to himself that what he really needed was a paycheck, and maybe a good, stiff drink.

*   *   *

The old man lay still in the small metal chair. A knowing smile flashed across his aged face, and then just as quickly, was gone again. His heart had dried up in his sagging chest decades earlier. It was now no more than a withered lump of tissue, a desiccated hunk of useless muscle which was incapable of love or emotion. The loss of his beloved wife Grace in a terrible house fire back in 1967 proved to be a pivotal point in his sad excuse for a life, and he never fully recovered from it.

A small ornate mirror hung on the far wall reflecting the interior of the drab, sparsely decorated room and its lone occupant. The old man watched it intently. He marveled at how such a small, simple furnishing could expand a room and all those in it.

Struggling to get up out of the chair, he kept a feeble grip on his afghan. He'd grown attached to the blanket over the years; his wife had stitched it for him decades earlier, shortly before her death, and it was one of the few reminders he still had of her.

His bones felt like driftwood and his joints like sandpaper, but the old man continued to plod slowly across the sterile, tiled floor of the generic nursing home room. He intended to reach the mirror and study his visage yet again in a vain, and most likely futile, attempt to reconcile with his very soul, his humanity, or whatever was left of it.

An instrumental, free-form jazz tune from Dave Koz drifted down the hallway from an overhead loudspeaker. It irritated the old man, temporarily hindering his concentration. He hated that type of music, and most of the staff at the home knew it. He preferred Benny Goodman or John Coltrane, or even Miles Davis. Now that was real music, not squeaky-clean imitators like they played nowadays.

"That moron Benson and his partners in crime are responsible for that noise pollution," he grumbled to himself. "How can I concentrate on my studies with all of that racket going on?"

No one was in the room to answer him. Only a warm breeze from a small window across the room made any sound.

"Punks. They'll pay. They'll all pay dearly."

Dragging his aged body over to the mirror, the old man lifted his head up level to it and gazed into his reflection. A bitter, resentful relic stared back at him. An old man who had lost all of his compassion for humanity, all his caring for the well-being of others, all of the love in his heart. He had grown indifferent to the suffering of others, only desiring that which would make him ascend to higher levels, to surpass the frail shell which God had inflicted on him. He only wanted to prove to the world, and to himself, that he was capable of more…of so much more.

With great effort he reached into his robe pocket and withdrew a small, pink mushroom. A sly, devious grin stretched across his wrinkled face as he studied it.

The gills of the growth were white, crowded together, and very finely attached to the upper stalk. A light blue, membranous partial veil of tissue extended from the edge of the cap to the upper stalk, covering the gills somewhat. A faint spore print of lavender dots decorated the cap.

The old man grunted in satisfaction at his unusual prize. He raised the growth up to his eye level, tilting it this way and that in his arthritic hand.

"Well hello there, my little friend," he said to the mushroom. "How's my favorite little guy doing today?"

The growth started to shake violently in his hand, eliciting a sigh of contentment from the old man. It pulsed with impossible movement, gyrating in his palm and oozing a translucent secretion from its cap, which coated the old man's hand and dripped onto the tiled floor, pooling at his slippered feet.

"That's a good boy," he sneered. "Let's begin our work again shall we?"

The mushroom settled into a rhythmic motion. It continued excreting the foul substance from its cap, but generally subsided somewhat, like a kitten having its ears scratched. The stalk then started to lengthen, lifting the cap with it, thinning the gills to the point of breaking, but not quite.

In fact, the gills then started to increase in girth and number, the new tissue forming a thick, nearly whole membrane under the mushroom's cap.

The old man's face tightened with anxious excitement. "That's right," he whispered. "That's very good."

Outside the window the wind was picking up. Trees wavered in the breeze, an aspect of the weather that the old man was overjoyed to see.

"You know what to do, my little friend. Let's send out another good dose, shall we. Do your magic for me again."

The mushroom then began to lift from the old man's hand. It hung in mid- air for a few seconds before rising, eventually suspended a full foot and a half above the old man's outstretched hand. On its cap the spore prints deepened in color. They gradually changed from a faint lavender hue to an angry, swirling mauve.

The old man watched as one of the spots rose up from the cap and began to rotate, spinning off its unusual, green -tinged color in a fine mist. The tiny droplets then flitted up and straight out of the window, scattering as soon as they hit the open air.

The old man flopped to the hard floor, ignoring the painful protests from his frail body. His heart and soul fell to the floor with him. Remorse for what he'd done, and for what he would still do, tapped on his mind. It wanted to gain entry, but he denied it, firmly locking the door, refusing to see any visitors.

The mushroom eventually conformed back to its original shape and form. The stalk shortened, the spore prints faded back to their original color, the cap shrunk and softened. And then the strange growth fell from the old man's hand and landed with a soft thud on the tiled floor.

Silence crept into the room. Outside the small window the wind settled back down to a light breeze. A line of sparrows soared by over the treetops.

The body of the old man lay prostrate across the floor, a slight trickle of blood leaking from the corners of his mouth. He was already beginning to feel the all-too familiar hunger yet again. It was gnawing at his mind and body.

He gleefully released his very soul into the ecstasies it offered.

His belly twisted in ravenous desire, desire for nourishment, desire to complete his fate. He had grown power hungry over the years, more so after the mushroom-like growth had drifted into his room on that cool September day the year before.

He bent over the mushroom, tearing into the pliable tissue of the growth with his toothless maw. Gray-colored gums mashed down onto the cap, churning the horrible mixture into a greasy pulp, which he swallowed in joyous gratification.

*   *   *

Cliff sauntered down the hallway. His Walkman headphones were spitting classic rock melodies into his ears. He tapped his fingers along to the driving drum beat and surrealistic bombasts of Ted Nugent's rock opus *Stranglehold.*

"Got you in a Stranglehold baby, you best get out of the way."

The stainless-steel cart he was pushing squeaked with every step he took, but Cliff didn't hear it. He was lost in Nugent's bizarre lyrics and powerful, flowing melody. His head swung back and forth, up and down, temporarily oblivious to where he was. But the music couldn't hide the fact that he was nearing Room C-3.

Cliff caught a quick glimpse of the room number between tufts of his hair. A polished chrome plate rimmed with red plastic displayed C-3 boldly. It was affixed next to the door, about shoulder height.

Cliff stopped abruptly in the hallway. He knew that C-3 was where the weird old man was, and that shadow as well, that twisted shape he saw earlier, or thought he saw. He did a quick one -eighty and scurried back down the corridor the way he came. He made a brief mental note to himself to look into exactly who the old man in C-3 was. He'd see Jane in the front office. She owed him a favor or two, notably when he covered for her in the past.

And behind him a dark shadow danced on the wall across from room C-3. It was in the shape of someone bent over. Someone eating something from the floor.

CHAPTER 8

Ryan lifted the hinged access door to the attic. Dust immediately swirled around, stinging his eyes and making him cough uncontrollably. He tried to prop the door open, wedging a screwdriver between it and one of the hinges, but the spring-loaded closer latch on it kept pulling it shut. He made a mental note to himself to remove the latch at a later time.

The spring and hinges groaned in protest as the door was raised, sending a hollow echo into the attic, and another mental note promptly wrote itself in Ryan's mind. The cheap pine shelves which lined the closet were flimsy at best. The former owner of the house had obviously installed them themselves. Ryan guessed that they weren't carpenters. The shelves were held up by thin, tarnished brackets; they couldn't have cost more than a dollar or two each, and the paint was peeling away in many places, revealing splintered, warped wood beneath. The shelves barely had enough strength to support a child, much less a young man like Ryan.

Gingerly planting first his left foot, then his right on the nearest plank Ryan began to slowly lower himself out of the attic. The six-foot, stainless-steel stepladder which stood at attention approximately two and a half feet below the lowest shelf patiently awaited its owner's foot.

"Man, I knew I should've got an eight foot ladder," Ryan lamented. "It was only a couple of bucks more."

The corpse of Wade Boulter bumbled its way through the rest of its property, occasionally knocking over a lawn chair or potted plant. The prize tulips that he had planted earlier in the season, his former life's pride and joy, were trampled under his ragged feet. Bright yellow petals quickly became flattened residue, coated in muck. Stems snapped. Delicate leaves fell. Beautiful, natural colors vanished.

Wade craned his neck up to the upper floor of his neighbor's house. The noise that had attracted his attention in the first place had for the most part stopped, but he still smelled the blood. Its rich, coppery aroma was strong, sparking a hint of past foggy memories in his rapidly decaying brain, such as the time he nearly sliced his thumb off while working in his garage. The blood had flowed freely then, splashing onto the epoxy floor, beading into innumerable red dots. The smell of his blood drifted into his nose then as well, mixing with the various chemicals and cleaners one would find in a garage.

The six-foot maple privacy fence that served as a property line between the two yards proved to be no match for the undead determination of Wade Boulter. With little effort he plowed through the wooden structure, the same one he himself had installed the previous summer. It was a solid, split-rail wood fence with rough and rugged posts and rails, and it made a compelling backdrop for his plantings. But now he smashed through it like it was so many cords of firewood.

Jagged chunks of varnished maple sliced into his palms and forearms, but he didn't cry out. He did not make any attempt to remove the pieces of wood. He merely glanced down at his wounds for a moment and continued onward, making his way toward his true destination: the house next door.

Ryan stood still for a second on the top rung of the stepladder. He thought he heard something, something that sounded like wood being smashed. He stood on the ladder, holding his breath, concentrating on the sound. He was puzzled as to what it might be, and became even more confused when the noise was replaced with other sounds: bushes being ransacked and rummaged through, weird grunts and moans, strange shuffling sounds. It sounded like someone was in his neighbor's yard, somebody no doubt making a big mess of things.

Ryan glanced around the closet searching for something to defend himself if need be. He eventually settled for the screwdriver he'd used to prop the attic access door open. His phone was on the other side of the house, so if he needed to call for help, he'd have to make his way to it; he'd feel safer with a weapon in his hands.

The sounds were getting closer now, and Ryan knew that whatever was making them was heading straight for him. That whatever it was sensed where he was hiding, and would stop at nothing to get to him.

Sweat began to bead on his forehead. His normally thick, curly hair was now matted to his scalp, damp with perspiration. He reached up and pulled the dangling string which promptly clicked off the light in the closet. Darkness swallowed the room and the lone occupant standing in it.

Not wanting to move, but sensing he needed to, Ryan stood perfectly still, wishing he had his handgun, or his Buck hunting knife, or a rake, or a shovel, or anything to properly arm himself with.

The screwdriver was laughing at him. It was making fun of him for choosing it as a weapon. Ryan responded by tightening his grip on the small tool. Imagination was a powerful thing, but it could also be a dangerous foe.

A cat meowed in the distance. Ryan struggled to place a face on the cat, but couldn't in his current state of mind.

Was it the neighbor's cat? Was it a stray? Or perhaps it was his. Wait, that's not it. He didn't have a cat. He was allergic to the dander.

A lump formed in Ryan's throat when he heard other more violent sounds, and the poor cat squealing in pain before its cries were abruptly cut off. Silence dominated again, and then the foraging noises continued, drawing closer and closer all the time.

Ryan decided that courage was the best weapon he could have. After all, he wasn't a kid anymore. He owned his own house now, had a dead end but relatively good paying job at Tomm's Hardware Outlet; he even had a little bit of money saved up and was contemplating tossing most of it into a Certificate of Deposit at Cant Bank.

A loud crash startled Ryan from his meandering thoughts. The noise was frightening, not only because of its sudden nature and intensity, but also due to the fact that it originated from his own backyard. In fact, it seemed to be right on his back patio.

Quick flashes of exactly what he had on his patio whisked through Ryan's mind. He attempted to fasten onto an image of possibilities of whoever was smashing their way across his yard.

His potted plants? No, the noises sounded like something metal was being destroyed.

His brand new Schwinn Searcher Supercross bike came to

mind as a possible victim. The mere thought of the aluminum trail-tuned framed and six-degree bend handlebar created a terse smile on his face, one that was tainted by the thought of any possible damage to it. But he had it tethered on the side of the house, not the patio. He wanted to have it prepped for his weekly ride up toward Addison Oaks, near Highland Hills.

And then he knew what it was.

It was his barbeque. His brand new barbeque with triple level, stainless steel cooking grates and cherry red, baked-on enamel finish.

Anger surged through Ryan, energizing his body in adrenalin-induced tension. How dare somebody damage his property. He'd show them whose house it was. He paid his taxes and his mortgage. He had rights.

Gripping the screwdriver tightly in his sweaty palm, Ryan stepped down the remaining rungs of the ladder, and navigating his way through the darkness, walked out of the closet.

Wade's corpse approached the doorwall. His ragged reflection in the glass stared back at him, pleading to be recognized, but he ignored it. He smelled the blood and wouldn't be denied. That was all that mattered to him. That and the powerful urges he was feeling that had nothing to do with hunger, or killing, or ending his suffering. No, these feelings that Wade felt were on a whole new level of understanding. They were absolute in their message, taking no prisoners, no rejection to their demands. All who heard them simply obeyed without question or delay.

Wade struggled to resist, but he knew it would eventually prove futile. It was simply a fact of his new existence, one which had no alternative.

The reflection in the doorwall glass reared back its rotting arms and in one violent lunge smashed through the window and into the interior of the house.

Ryan froze in the hallway, his heart racing in his chest. He quickly substituted his Louisville slugger Black Beauty baseball bat for the screwdriver (fortunately he'd left it near his bedroom door- an unusual advantage to being a bachelor living alone). He leaned forward slightly, attempting to see down the corridor as much as he could, but only managed to make out vague outlines of bedroom and bathroom doors. Since he didn't want to turn on any lights, it was the price he had to pay. Surprise and stealth might just prove to be valuable weapons if he was confronted with an intruder.

The racket coming from his family room was tightening his stomach in knots. Somebody was definitely in his house and obviously couldn't care less if they were heard or not. This only frightened Ryan even more; paralysis threatened to freeze him where he stood.

But another emotion, one that could be just as strong as fear was also seeping into his mind...anger. He was getting really ticked off that somebody had the nerve to break into his house. If someone had the ability and time to do a crime then they could've also used those attributes to get a job and earn an honest living. Laziness was something that he absolutely detested. There was simply no excuse for it.

With newfound determination, Ryan flipped the hallway light switch on and stomped down the hallway, heading straight for the family room...and whoever was waiting there for him.

CHAPTER 9

Sam straightened up after getting his fill of water. His mind played with all the possibilities of what he should do, of what he could do next.

Continue working on Mrs. Ether's Ford? He would be able to have it done for her within a couple of hours or so. But the thought of crawling back underneath a ton and a half of automobile and digging his hands into rusted nuts and bolts didn't really appeal to him.

So without giving it another thought Sam walked past the vehicles in Feeter's Automobile Repair Haven, and their propped open hoods, and partially disassembled motors and transmissions. He sauntered by the scattered tools and the rows and rows of dangling air filters and fan belts. He paused momentarily to gawk at Miss July hanging on the wall, but then passed her by as well, although her attractive, sexy smile wavered in his mind for a short while afterwards.

Where ya think you're going? the leering image of his father asked. The face was plastered across the driver's side door of a nearby Chevrolet sedan. Specks of grime and dust dotted the expression of his dad. Sam stopped in mid-step and peered over at the face. Without warning he let a howling laugh escape. It resonated off the automotive supplies.

"I'm gonna do what I should have done a while ago," he said with satisfaction. "I'm gonna hang up my wrench and my hammer, and my screwdriver, and my socket set, and I'm going outside for a much needed breath of fresh air. I'm going to let the sun warm my face. I'm going to let the breeze blow through my hair. I'm going to let my mind wander through nature's garden."

The image of Sam's father snickered, its face twisting in disgust and disappointment. *Whatever. You'll lose your job ya know. Feeter will be plenty mad about your so-called journey to find yourself, or whatever it is you call it.* The face smiled sharply, an *I- told -you- so* look on its face. *And if you don't believe me, you can go right ahead and ask Old Man Feeter for yourself.*

46

The strange reply caught Sam off-guard. What did he mean ask him himself? Feeter had left for the day. Sam had seen Feeter's silver Monte Carlo pull away from the shop.

Or did he?

Sam turned and scanned the side parking area where his boss usually parked his car. The space was empty but the spot next to it wasn't. A chill seized his spine as he focused on the custom license plate on the silver Monte Carlo. *Da Boss* was printed in bold, old English letters, clear as a bell.

Spinning around, Sam's gaze immediately fell on the window to Mr. Feeter's office. The ragged corpse of his boss was standing in it. A baleful hunger was prominent in his dead eyes, bloody smears and bits of human tissue across his face.

"No! It can't be! It was only my hallucinations! It was only my mind playing tricks on me!"

Sam grasped for a plausible explanation, something logical to fasten the impossible scene before him onto: neglecting to take his medication properly, working too hard, the effects of the grimy, stale air in the shop, anything which made at least a shred of common sense. Anything at all.

Sam spun around, frantically searching for his father's face on the wall, but it wasn't there. Only the typical mess of tools and assorted discarded car parts one would find in a repair shop could be seen.

I told you so boy, his father's voice stated in a no-nonsense tone from no particular source. *I told you that your boss wouldn't be happy with you walking out on the job. I told you so.* A thin but definite undertone of biting sarcasm laced every single word.

Sam felt the cold, dead breath of Mr. Feeter on the back of his neck. Feeter's body didn't need to breath; it was just a reflex that he still adhered to. A bizarre remnant of his former existence. Pain reared its ugly head.

And with lightening quick speed, Feeter reared back and unleashed a vicious series of blows at Sam, some missing completely, some connecting with devastating results.

Sam reeled backwards, nearly losing his balance. But he braced himself against a wall as small, various sized boxes of oil filters rained down on top of him. His head spun and his legs buckled. His eyes watered. He wanted his mother. He wanted, dare he think it, his father. He needed his medication; it would make the nightmares go away.

But this was no nightmare. This was no hallucination. What he was experiencing was not caused by any medical condition. This was real, in all its bloody, terrifying glory.

More from instinct than from anything else, Sam immediately started groping for something, anything to throw at the creature. He reached back, his eyes locking on the parting mouth and blackened gums and teeth advancing toward him, and one after another threw with all his remaining strength every single item he laid his hands on.

Boxes, papers, nuts, bolts, socket heads, oil rags, wrenches, all flew into the dead face of Mr. Feeter. The grisly corpse threw up its hand out of instinct, not because of possible injury. It grunted in frustration, heaving distorted curses, and groans at Sam.

Sam realized that his best chance for escape was right then and there. The small window of opportunity that was afforded to him did not allow the luxury of hesitation or indecision.

Sam dropped the partially dismantled alternator he was about to throw and turned to run for his life. He'd worry about what Feeter was or why he wanted to kill him later. Priorities insisted that staying alive was number one on the list.

The alternator clanked to the floor, echoing in the shop. Sam didn't look back. He darted straight for the sliding glass door, the same one he rolled Mrs. Ether's Ford through the day before, sauntering in and out without thinking twice about it. Now it was an escape route that would save his life. A portal to freedom, to fresh air and sunshine, to safety from the hideous nightmare in the shop.

But then something very strange caught his attention. Feeter had turned away from him and was stumbling in the opposite direction, heading back toward the shredded wall of his office.

Was he going back to finish his meal in his office? With no regard for any injuries he might suffer as a result, Sam's dead boss plowed straight through the remains of his office wall.

The racket pierced Sam's ears, further heightening his already disoriented state of mind. Wallboard dust and flaked latex paint swirled in the shop. Jagged shards of glass scattered to the floor to join the other debris, remnants of two -by- four wooden studs crumbled into unrecognizable splinters. And with one violent lunge, Feeter barreled through what was left of the wall and into his trashed office.

Sam fought the urge to follow his boss, to try to understand why one minute the corpse was crashing through walls to get him and the next minute practically running away. Ignoring the cautious part of his mind, Sam slowly walked over to Feeter's office and peered inside. He just caught a glimpse of the corpse swinging open the rear door of the office and quickly darting out of it, a sickly trail of blood in its wake.

Sam surveyed the office. A sad feeling settled over him. Such destruction and fear running rampant without boundaries to contain or monitor it. The world was full of such sadness, such evil. Sam had experienced small doses of it when he lived at home with his parents. His arguments with his father, his battles with his state of mind, his lack of any real direction in his life. But these problems paled in comparison to the frightening mess that was before his weary eyes.

Virtually every piece of furniture was at the very least upturned, at the worst, smashed beyond recognition. Pictures of Feeter in his earlier days: holding up a large mouth bass, sitting with his wife in some far off exotic vacation spot, standing in front of Feeter's Automotive Repair Haven shortly after it opened; these and others, a veritable scrapbook to his life, were either lying on the floor smashed or dangling precariously at twisted, sharp angles, ready to fall at the slightest touch.

Feeter's desk, his solid mahogany desk with leather inlays and custom, extra deep drawers, was on its side, cast aside like a stack of firewood. Several file cabinets were also tipped over, drawers gaping open, dozens of papers and folders scattered across the floor. Sam stepped into the room cautiously, slowly, ever aware of potential dangers. Even though he'd seen Feeter leave the building, he still wasn't sure what might still be lurking about.

He smelled it before he saw it. A thick, pungent stench that could not be mistaken for anything other than was it was….a dead body. Or more accurately Tim's Feeter's body.

The teenage boy's lifeless corpse was sprawled in impossible ways. His legs were bent in ninety- degree angles facing away from each other. His torso was twisted to Sam's right, his head (or what was left of it) was bent toward Sam's left. Sam hadn't seen anything so horrible in his life, and he found himself thinking of the Saturday morning cartoons he used to watch when he was a kid. Animated characters being flattened by falling anvils and pianos, getting hit over the head with giant hammers and clubs, being run over by trains and cars.

But those were cartoons, fun and colorful shows designed to make fun of dangerous situations. What lay open and bleeding before Sam's disbelieving eyes was not a cartoon character. It was a person, a human being who had hopes and dreams. Who had thoughts, fears, worries, and desires. And now it was nothing more than a discarded heap of bloody tissue and fat, gristle, bone, internal organs and flesh. There were no more dreams. No more imagination. No more aspirations. Sam was raised to believe in God, and that there was something else after death. He believed that the soul, a person's personality, the heart, and possibly even the mind itself, departed the body and went somewhere beyond understanding.

But as he stared down at Tim's remains, he felt tiny slivers of doubt creep into his mind.

Why don't you go and follow that boss man of yours, Son?

"Leave me alone, Dad. I have enough on my mind already."

That's my boy, Sam. Never any good at coping with life or what it throws at you.

The face glanced down at the corpse. *Or what Death throws at you either.*

Sam ignored the comment and stepped over the still, cold body. He navigated his way across the mess in the room to the back door which Mr. Feeter had stumbled through, and walked into the warm breeze outside. He was going to follow Mr. Feeter's corpse and see just where it was heading.

Sam pulled the door closed behind him, more out of habit than necessity. And in the trashed office, the body of Tim Feeter began to twitch.

CHAPTER 10

Jerry held his breath. Just the thought of what he was about to confront made him sick to his stomach. He thanked God he hadn't eaten anything in a while; this wasn't the time to vomit all over himself.

'Is that you Jerry, Honey?" Stephanie's corpse teased from the kitchen. "I know very well it is. Why don't you come in here, Honey, and give me a hand?"

Give her a hand? Help her with what?

"Oh, very well then, you old sourpuss. If you won't give me a hand, you can have one of mine then."

The implications the words held were more than any sane person could endure. Jerry braced himself for the inevitable, and it came.

The left hand of Stephanie, still wearing the three-quarter carat diamond wedding ring that Jerry had placed on her finger twenty years earlier, came spiraling through the opening in the wall and landed with a sickening, wet thud at his feet. Jerry stepped back in revulsion, nearly tripping on the blackened blood oozing from the severed hand. Stephanie let loose with deep guttural laughter which echoed throughout the house. And then all fell silent.

Jerry stood perfectly motionless. He knew Stephanie was still there but for some reason she was not moving at all. Only the steady ticking of the wall clock punctuated the silence.

Quickly searching the laundry room for anything to arm himself, Jerry focused on one of the few items which had any potential: Stephanie's steam iron.

It was a Panasonic with jet stream holes and was fairly heavy for an iron. And it was perfect, just what he needed. Something with weight to it and even a sharp- pointed edge. He had no intention of getting close enough to his dead wife to utilize that aspect of the small appliance, but it reassured his mind to know it was there nonetheless. Just in case.

He snatched the iron from its base on the wall above the utility sink. If only he would be able to heat the iron first, thus adding another dimension to his weaponry. But he quickly dismissed the notion due to the simple and all too real possibility that Stephanie could come barging through the doorway, or even the wall itself.

The iron felt cold and solid in his hand. Holding it behind his head, Jerry tiptoed toward the doorway leading into the kitchen. He resisted the urge to pinch his nose (the smell of rot was thick in the air), instead settling for a wadded up piece of discarded paper towel.

"Stephanie?" he called out in a tone barely above a whisper. "Stephanie? It's me, Jerry. We need to talk."

A shadow in the kitchen moved, bumping into something, perhaps the counter or stove, and stumbled away from Jerry.

Was she trying to leave?

This question, along with a host of others, swirled around in his head. Each and every one vied for attention, as all were undoubtedly worthy of it.

Jerry decided to implement his *Double Q* approach again. It had never failed him before and he was confident it wouldn't now. He slid up to the doorway and peered into the kitchen in one swift movement. The iron was held ready in his hand by white knuckles, the cord trailing to the floor behind him.

The first thing he saw was the mess: smashed plates and glasses, spilled, rotted food, numerous pots and pans tumbled over from their normal hanging location above the center island. The house was destroyed; it was a broken mass of plastic, glass, and metal, and Jerry wished he remembered just where he left his cell phone, although he was sure the battery was dead by then.

And then he saw her.

It was Stephanie. She was turned away from him, the back of her head slick with blood, and slowly made her way out of the kitchen, heading toward the twin French doors which led into the small isolated dining room. From there, Jerry surmised, she would go straight through the other door in the dining room and hang a quick right and out the front door. Just exactly where she would go after she left the house, Jerry couldn't even begin to guess. Or want to for that matter.

Jerry stood perfectly still, trying not to breathe, trying not to blink. Part of his heart ached to run over to Stephanie and embrace her right then and there. She had been the woman he loved, his soul mate, the mother of his children.

His children?

The horrifying recollection of his youngest attacking him played itself out in his frayed mind over and over again. Each memory brought with it a fresh batch of pain and fear.

Jerry snapped back to the present. He forced himself to suppress the heartache he felt for his children; after all, he had enough to worry about as it was.

Stephanie was oblivious to her husband standing nearby. She pushed the French doors open, the stump where her hand had been leaving a sickly tail of gore behind her. Jerry found himself staring at the terrible wound on his wife. He felt ashamed of himself, feeling like someone slowing down to view a car accident, one in which it was obvious there were fatalities.

And in the next instant Stephanie was stumbling out the front door, leaving a trail of clotted blood and many future nightmares behind her. She weaved around the potted flowers and hanging plants that in life she had cared for so deeply, but now were nothing more than nuisances, obstacles, hindrances to her mysterious journey and its unknown destination.

She swatted aside the plants and kicked the flowers out of her way. Soft grunts of satisfaction slipped past her cracked lips and escaped into the early morning air. Jerry stealthily scooted to the bay window in the dining room and watched what was left of his beloved wife walking away from their home, from their children, from their life together.

The burning thirst Jerry felt suddenly reared its ugly head at him at that moment, demanding to be recognized, to be slated or vowed there would be dire consequences to pay. Dehydration was nothing to trifle with, particularly in someone in such a state as he was.

As fast as his weak legs would carry him, Jerry raced to the kitchen faucet, pushed the lever up and buried his head under the cool, wet flow of the filtered water. He lapped up the life-saving liquid like a dog, momentarily losing himself in the refreshing ecstasy it offered.

His thirst quenched, he then wolfed down anything edible nearby that wasn't noticeably spoiled. He stuffed slices of rye bread, saltine wheat crackers, and vanilla crème cookies into his mouth, anything that he could get his hands on. The snacks meshed into a frenzied mush in his mouth.

And then, noticing the clock on the wall and how much time had elapsed since Stephanie had stumbled out of the house, Jerry sprinted to his bedroom and retrieved his handgun from the top of the closet. The thought of putting a bullet through his wife's head sent a sharp chill up and down his spine, but he vowed to himself he would do it if he had to. She wasn't alive anymore, at least not in the sense of a living, breathing, loving person. She was a thing, an inhuman monster, a zombie of some sort bent on his, and probably anybody else's she came across, destruction…or worse.

Stuffing a few bottles of water and various snacks and cookies into his duffle bag, Jerry sprinted out the front door, being careful to avoid any residue from Stephanie that she had left behind. He thought of calling for help but decided against it, at least not yet. First he wanted to find his wife.

He gripped the storm door's handle tightly, and yet without much conviction. He wanted to turn it. He needed to turn it. But he still found it to be a difficult thing to do. The realization that it could quite possibly be the last time he would set foot in his home settled over him, sapping whatever strength he had left, diluting any happy memories. He knew he must follow Stephanie.

"Goodbye," was all he said to the empty house. And with a quick jerk of his wrist, walked out the front door and began his pursuit. Martin was on his mind as well, but Stephanie just might lead him to a solution to this nightmare. As much as it pained him to admit it, that was more important than finding his last surviving child. The entire fate of mankind might hinge on what answers he could find.

CHAPTER 11

It drove Janice Arron crazy sometimes when all her husband seemed to want to do was lock himself away in their garage and tinker with his Chevy Camaro. Lately it was all he did. She wondered how much someone could do to a car. You could only change parts on it, wax it, and tune up the engine so much. Eventually he'd run out of things to do to it.

The noises kept her up at night. Wrenches clanking against other wrenches, metal pipes banging into other metal pipes, power tools grinding away, the high-pitched whirl of the moving parts ringing in her ears and echoing throughout her house; these sounds were annoyingly constant.

It was that stupid car that did it. That dark blue and red monstrosity that was serving as a wedge being driven directly between her and her wonderful husband Pat.

Lord knows she'd confronted him in the past about it. How he spent far too much time working on the car. How he never took her out anymore. How even their own daughter felt distanced from her father at times.

But Pat would never listen to her, or he would for a short while and then gradually, inevitably, slide back to his garage, and his tools, and his 1983 Camaro, or whatever the heck kind of car it was.

"Pat? Pat? Honey, are you there?" A burst of anger crossed Janice's pale face. She hated it when he locked the door to the garage. Sometimes she even wondered if he did it just to spite her.

She called out again and again, her fleshy palms slapping against the cold steel of the garage door. "Pat? Patrick Richard Arron, you answer me right now! Do you hear me? Right now!"

She did her best to temper her impatience, but knew it was a losing battle. She saw the glow from the fluorescent lights inside the garage leaking through the curtains on a nearby window so she knew he was in there. She also heard Buddy Holly crooning *"That'll be the day, when I die"* from the garage. How Pat loved those old 50's classic rock tunes.

After five minutes with no response, Janice's anger was gradually being replaced with worry. She decided her only option was to make her way to the window, which although small and skirted with thick curtains, might allow her to peek into the garage.

It was when Janice pressed her face to the windowpane that two things struck her as odd.

First: the thin, greenish film all over her hands, her face, the window glass. She didn't notice it initially, but when she did, it froze her blood.

And second: the still form of her husband lying underneath his car. Several thin streams of crimson spread out from his body, pooling into a circular puddle around a small floor drain in the center of the garage floor.

Terror whacked Janice hard in her gut. Was he all right? Why was there blood on the floor? And what was that strange greenish film over everything?

She plucked a decorative stone from a nearby flowerbed and immediately pitched it straight through the garage window. The rock landed with a thud and rolled to a stop right next to Pat's form.

He didn't move…at first.

Janice was screaming hysterically, feverishly, throwing anything she could get her hands on into the window. She had to widen the opening so she could crawl through to get to Pat. In the confused, panic-stricken maelstrom of her mind, she didn't think to retrieve her cell phone, or get a neighbor, or even yell for help. All that registered in her head was reaching Pat.

Fueled by adrenalin, Janice hoisted herself up and crawled through the window, cutting her palms on the residual pieces of glass still jutting up in the frame.

Pat lay motionless not more than ten feet away from his frantic wife. His beloved Camaro was on top of him, two pitted chrome wheel stands on their side, thick, jagged cracks running through them. Pat had been the unfortunate victim of a bizarre accident, one caused by faulty equipment and improper safety precautions. It happens, but never to someone like Pat Arron. He was always a staunch believer in safety.

Janice heard the first noise as she was attempting to lower herself down onto a long workbench under the window. The sound instantly raised hope that her husband was still alive, but quickly receded into fear when she realized what was causing the noise.

Pat was lifting the car up off of himself. His bent and broken arms raised the 3400 lb. vehicle up like a bench press. The sounds of bones fracturing echoed in the stale, green mist tinted air.

Janice fell to the floor, and twisted her ankle in the process. Pat tossed the Camaro aside and sat upright, blood leaking from his smashed face and head. Janice screamed even louder. Pat stood up and approached his hysterical wife. His features had been reduced to a bloody pulp, his shoulders flattened, his arms bent at impossible angles.

"H…hello dear," he mumbled through shattered teeth and an evil grin "I smelled your blood." The thing that had been Janice's husband shambled forward on broken legs, advancing slowly, methodically, confident in its ability to use fear to its advantage.

And when the zombie finished with Janice, it gave into the overwhelming urges punctuating its smashed brain. It stumbled out of the garage door and into its destiny.

*   *   *

Jane thumbed through the stacks and stacks of papers. The large file cabinet stood silently before her, its top drawer slid open to reveal its contents. Several snapshots of various family members adorned its sides.

"Uhh, let's see," she mumbled with a bored look on her face. "Which room did you say it was again?"

Cliff rolled his eyes. He never cared for Jane that much, and only endured her as a co-worker, an unavoidable aspect of his job. "C 3," he repeated for what felt like the hundredth time. "He's an old guy, been here probably for the better part of ten years or so."

Jane nodded while flipping through the files.

"Why don't you just punch it in on the computer?" Cliff asked; impatience was seeping into his voice.

"Sometimes it's easier to do things the old-fashioned way. Besides that old piece of junk needs an overhaul. Just last week alone it crashed on me twice. Had to re-file all the patients and reinstall every single program. It took me forever."

Cliff rolled his eyes again.

"Here we are, Room C-3. Mr. Preston. Mr. Grady Preston. He's been here…actually I'm not sure just when he arrived. It's like he's just always been here."

Cliff straightened up. "He's always been here?"

"According to our files. No family. No friends. No visitors. Nothing."

"How can that be? Who pays for him then? How'd he get here?"

Jane slid the yellowed file back into the drawer and promptly closed it. It clicked loudly in the small office.

"Sometimes that happens," she answered with a smirk. "The State takes care of them as far as I know." And then she sat back down behind her cluttered desk without another word and continued tapping on the computer keyboard.

Cliff left the front office confused and worried. He'd run into a dead end and frankly didn't know where else to turn. How could he avoid Mr. Grady Preston?

*   *   *

The old man felt better than he had in days. His back pain had diminished almost completely and the aches and pains which usually accompanied his every movement had receded considerably. He felt like a new man. A new man with a purpose, a mission that he was looking forward to fulfilling.

"I'm an actor," he mused to the empty room. "I'm a world-famous actor who is about to take the stage for his finest performance. A presentation worthy of the world's recognition." His wrinkled face took on a malicious slant. "And indeed the world will notice my performance. Of this I can personally guarantee."

The old man felt strong enough to stand upright, and despite his worrisome nature, threw caution to the wind and lifted himself up off the cold tile floor of his room. True, he'd grown somewhat accustomed to the place: the full-sized mattress surrounded by stainless-steel bedposts, the clean but painfully sterile bathroom with virtually no leg space or vanity, the rectangular double-paned window which offered a bland view consisting of one part elm and birch trees and two parts elm and birch trees. All in all, it was a veritable paradise; that is if he were a homeless man.

With renewed purpose, the old man straightened up and surveyed the room as if for the first time. He sensed he was finished with it, much like a toddler would tire of a rubber ball. His greater purpose was beginning to root itself in his soul. He would travel above all else, and watch the past and future unfold before him. He would set the order for all subservient beings to follow and obey. He would see all. He would see as a god sees.

The old man's thoughts were interrupted. He sensed a new birth close by. Very close. His heightened senses were beginning to take hold. He could feel the soul departing the body, starting its journey upward to the heavens. He could smell the blood in the body ceasing its circulation, puddling in the low spots, beginning to clot and thicken. The organs were abandoned to their inevitable fate. The senses (sight, hearing, smell, touch and taste) fled like escaped prisoners from a penitentiary.

A stern, dry, medically professional voice chimed in from the loudspeakers in the hallway. The woman on the intercom, although undoubtedly hardened from years of medical emergencies and life-threatening situations, let a discernable tremble in her tone shine through.

"Doctor Mortoon to room B-14 please. Doctor Mortoon to room B-14 please."

The old man paused for a moment. The entire world stopped spinning for him in that instant, becoming a floating, lifeless rock in the black sea of outer space.

He waited.

Three minutes passed before the screaming started.

Echoing down the long hallway, the screams shattered the normally peaceful wanderings of the residents of Abby Convalescent Home. And with the screams came other noises as well. Inhuman noises of death, fear, and mindless hunger. Sounds which could only be coaxed from a human being if they were experiencing something horrible that should not be happening, but was. Something well beyond the boundaries of common sense.

A crooked smile split the old man's face. "Yes, sir," he croaked. "Mr. Grady Preston is gonna finally have his day." The smile faded into a frown. "If only my Grace was here to share it with me. If only."

The people rushing by his room in the hallway interrupted his train of thought. He recognized several of them: nurses, caretakers, a few fellow residents in the home; he couldn't help but notice that they all were in a frantic state. One, (Nurse Stacy Panta), an attractive dark-haired twenty- something who had administered his medicine in the past, was the last one to sprint by his doorway.
She was screaming her lovely head off. Obviously something was chasing her and the others as well. Something quite frightening no doubt.

Grady watched and waited in twisted fascination for the antagonist to come rumbling down the hallway. He was anxious to see it for himself. Then he would know for sure that his life had not been wasted.

The zombie stumbled down the corridor, careening off walls as it moved like some bloodied pinball. It was impervious to the injuries it was sustaining, or perhaps it simply didn't care. Either way it was a mess.

It had been Mrs. Geraldine Baxter, an elderly woman who had recently become a grandmother for the first time. A faint, residual trace of joy of that fact still shone in her glazed-over eyes. She was after the nurses, or anybody else she could get a hold of. The brain aneurysm, which had caused her death, had come on suddenly, dropping her to the tiled floor of her room as she was reading a book. One minute she was thoroughly engrossed within the printed passages of Stephen King's post-apocalyptic horror classic *The Stand*, and the next minute she was flat-lining. In the end she was all alone in death, just as everyone is.

As the doctor and other medical professionals leaned over her rapidly-cooling body, Mrs. Geraldine Baxter, new grandmother, avid fan of Stephen King, and resident of Abby Convalescent Home, suddenly came to, effectively swatting aside the very people who were trying to save her life. She leaped to her slippered feet and promptly sunk her yellowed teeth into the nearest person, a portly, mild-mannered man named Levon, who had only been working at the home for a mere two and a half months. She'd never worn dentures and the bite was strong and lethal.

Levon screamed for a second or two before his throat was completely ripped out, thus ending his dreams of a rhythm and blues singing career. And his life.

The other unfortunate people in Mrs. Baxter's room on that fateful day were either immediately and violently dispatched by her or were fleeing down the hallway for their lives.

Grady smiled to himself, the partially digested remains of the mushroom-like growth still churned in his shriveled stomach.

"It's started," he mused in a sly tone. "It's finally started. After all this time, it has finally started."

The hallway lights were flickering, giving the corridor an ominous look. Originating from Mrs. Baxter's room, the stains of red, spotted with chunks of viscera, smeared the floor and walls. It was a sickening testament to the horrors that occurred that day.

Grady walked to the door and nudged it the rest of the way open. He peered out into the hallway. An uneasy silence had settled over the grisly scene.

The first thing he noticed was two dead bodies propped against the opposite wall. He recognized one of them (a fellow resident whom he had talked with on occasion). Both had their throats torn out. Apparently neither had managed to escape the clutches of Mrs. Baxter. Something inexplicable compelled him to glare at the bloody carnage. He simply couldn't help himself. It was like driving by a bad car accident, one which you knew there were fatalities in. Most people would stare at the car wrecks, wondering, trying to catch a glimpse of an injured person, trying to see what had happened.

The floor of the hallway was sticky with pooling blood and it smelled of decay. But Grady was happy anyway. He perceived the mess as a trail, a type of map which would eventually lead him to his life's purpose.

Stepping out into the hallway, Grady quickly looked both ways. One side was empty, save for a few more inert bodies strewn against walls and lying on the floor. At the other end however was the creator of the slaughter: Mrs. Baxter.

The grandmotherly zombie paid the old man no heed. She plodded along, pulled toward a destination she didn't understand, but was powerless to resist. In her wrinkled hand she still held her book.

CHAPTER 12

Emily sauntered out of the laundry room, clothesbasket brimming with freshly washed towels. She was humming a Michael Jackson song she'd heard on the radio earlier that morning in the kitchen.

"*Cause this is Thriller, Thrill...*" She never understood just what the King of Pop was singing in the chorus of his classic tune.

She set the laundry basket down on the over-sized dining room table and began to remove the towels, folding each one neatly into tight, uniform squares. Images of decayed zombies dancing on a fog-shrouded, moonlit street to Jackson's catchy beat filtered into her head.

Those were the days. The 1980's. A time of rebellion, plastic outfits, purple and pink-spiked haircuts, and classic, souped-up muscle cars in every teenage boy's driveway. Yes, those were good days.

"Honey? Have you seen my red tie? You know, the one I wore to John and Melinda's wedding last month?"

"Mom! Tommy said I'm a big dummy because I can't spell my last name yet! Mom?"

The familiar voices in the house jarred Emily back to the present. The fresh, fun-filled days of the 1980's slipped away to mere memories once again.

Without answering the calls from her loved ones, Emily tossed the towel she was folding back into the basket and walked straight to the quiet sanctuary of her bedroom, never once looking back. Her unmade bed felt even more comfortable than it looked as she collapsed into it in relaxed bliss.

Sunlight streamed in through the dusty drapes, warming the room and illuminating the thousands of minute dust particles floating about. Even though Emily knew perfectly well the cleanest of homes were littered with dust, it still disgusted her. Without thinking about it, she shook her head vigorously, trying to clean the dust that might have settled in her hair.

The scream cut through the peaceful silence of the bedroom, effectively halting any frivolous thoughts about past eras or dust particles Emily had been entertaining. The sheer terror in the cry was amplified not only from its suddenness and intensity, but also by its origin.

Emily's youngest, her little princess, the child whom she looked forward to teaching how to apply makeup and how to experiment with the latest hairstyles, was screaming at the top of her little lungs. And Emily could also hear the heavy footfalls of her husband bounding across the house; he was running toward their daughter.

The clothesbasket tumbled to the floor as Emily sprinted out of the room. Her stomach was twisting in painful knots. Her head was spinning as it filled with terrifying images of possible tragic scenarios: a cut hand from a jagged piece of glass or metal, a twisted ankle, or a nasty bite from that bad-tempered dog next door, or worse, a spider! God how she hated spiders.

Emily was running through the house toward her daughter when she heard another cry. It was her son Tommy. His shrieking voice cracked through the air like a whip, sending additional shivers up and down her back like an electrical current.

And then, as if in some type of demented nightmare that kept escalating with each horrendous moment that passed, Emily heard her husband scream. And when she finally reached the living room she immediately realized that the cries that she had heard were not cries of fear, but of pain, agonizing pain.

Standing on the outskirts of the living room, Emily was motionless, mouth agape at the shocking scene before her. Her son Tommy, all seventy-five pounds of him, was standing beside the still forms of her little daughter and her husband. Both bodies were sheathed in blood, hideous strips of torn open flesh were raked across each one, strange green growths sprouting up from jagged wounds. Apparently Tommy had tripped while playing with his plastic army men and had hit his head on the edge of the coffee table. The four-inch long gash across his forehead attested to that fact. His skull was exposed through the wound, revealing the tough bone gleaming with trickles of blood and tissue; her fate was sealed.

When Tommy sensed that his mother was in the room, he turned to face her, his eyes clouded over and lifeless. He advanced on Emily very quickly. And behind him the corpses of his father and little sister began to sit upright.

A part of Emily didn't really care by that time. Her world had already ended with the deaths of her family. How she would die didn't really concern her that much. All she wanted was to join her husband and children in Heaven.

The three zombies then fell upon Emily, savaging catapulting her into oblivion.

*   *   *

Ryan crept closer and closer toward his family room. Morning sunlight streamed through the curtains, lighting just enough of the room with a greenish cast to where he could see. But not much. The baseball bat was feeling heavier in his hands, but it was also all he had at the moment. It could be the difference between life and death.

"I'm armed," he blurted out before he could help himself. "Get out of my house right now or I swear to God I'll take you out!"

No response. The silence was deafening.

Ryan stepped forward cautiously, wielding the baseball bat in front of him like a sword. Shadows hung on every wall despite the sun sneaking into the room. Ryan never felt so uncomfortable in his own house, and this feeling is what spawned the growing anger in him, a tidal wave of frustration and rage that wouldn't be denied or ignored.

He charged into the room, bat ready as if he were going to take a homerun swing in Game Seven of the World Series.

And then he stopped dead in his tracks.

The corpse of Wade Boulter stood next to Ryan's worn, secondhand leather couch. Streaks of rotten blood dripped down his neighbor's face and chest, and were splattered across the shards of broken glass on the floor.

"Ryan," the dead man drawled, "I need to talk to you. I'm afraid I might have damaged your property a little bit." As he spoke, trying his best to push aside the urges deep within his head, he was slowly but steadily advancing toward his young neighbor. A strong odor of death and decay drifted around the room.

Ryan stood motionless, transfixed by who, by what had broken into his house.

"I see you cut yourself," Wade smirked. His pallid brow creased with excitement. "I knew I smelled blood."

Ryan snapped to, and fueled from anger, launched himself at the zombie.

Wade, despite having only one eye, sidestepped Ryan in an instant and smacked him on the back of the head. The baseball bat fell as Ryan crashed to the floor, his palms skidding across pieces of glass.

Dazed from his fall, Ryan pushed himself up onto his elbows. Wade was standing over him, gripping his hair in a dead hand.

"And now," Wade rasped. "Time for the main course."

Ryan could feel the strength and power in the dead man's grip. It felt like his head, his whole body, was being hoisted up by a crane. He thrashed back and forth but to no avail, the zombie possessed some type of superhuman strength. Bloody spittle trickled down onto the back of Ryan's head as he heard the undead creature groaning in delight at its latest conquest.

But then, just as Ryan had resigned himself to his grisly fate, the grip of impending death suddenly released him, sending him spiraling back to the land of the living. A full two minutes passed before Ryan had the strength, or the nerve, to look up.

He watched in joyous disbelief as his neighbor, the man with a nice family, who was always banging away on his drums, stumbled out the way he came in, through the shattered doorwall, a sticky trail of bloody visceral in his wake.

Out into the backyard, Wade roamed. The pull enveloping him was absolute and unwavering. It was to be heeded without delay, a threat of immediate and utter oblivion its weapon. And Wade obeyed, his deteriorating body walking, crawling if necessary, to reach the destination pre-ordained for him.

Ryan stood in his family room, his lower back and head

screaming at him in protest. The clock on the wall ticked steadily along. The refrigerator in the kitchen hummed softly. A small blue jay chirped from a nearby tree branch. A distant bark from a dog down the street echoed.

Ryan took a deep breath as he watched the zombie ramble through his backyard and out into an unsuspecting world, a world which undoubtedly would not be prepared to accept or deal with such a threat. And a strange thought drifted into his mind. An old line from a popular, local horror author he used to read back in high school. The ominous line was a prelude to the only book the writer ever wrote:

Just because something is impossible doesn't mean that it can't happen.

The words had always sent a chill down Ryan's spine, not only because of the frightening passages that were sure to follow, but also from the underlying truth lurking within their meaning. Anything is possible, even impossible things. And now Ryan had experienced the impossible firsthand, in his very own house. And that same impossible had attacked him as well, nearly devouring him alive right in his own family room.

Reaching over and grasping his Louisville slugger baseball bat from the carnage of the room, Ryan stepped through the doorwall opening and began his dangerous trek.

CHAPTER 13

The absence of other people on the dusty roads of Toals Creek was immediately noticed by Sam. It reminded him of the old science fiction movies he used to sneak into when he was a kid at the Showcase Cinema movie theater up on Van Dyke. A tense smile slipped across his face. He half expected to see some random tumbleweed rolling across the empty streets.

A slight breeze was blowing in from the north, bringing with it a strange mixture of fresh- smelling pine trees and the foul stench of decay. Sam felt relieved in a way. Tracking Feeter might be a little easier than he had originally thought; it was a small consolation for all had been through, but at this point he'd take anything he could get.

Eyeing J.J.'s Party Store across the road, his grumbling stomach quickly made up his mind on where he would go next. He could call the sheriff from there as well. There was a phone back in the shop, but that was the last place he wanted to go. He just couldn't bring himself to look at Tim again.

The front door to J.J.'s store was practically wide open. Sam, puzzled by this, slipped into the store cautiously. He was thinking about finding some type of weapon by then as well as food. He'd need both to survive.

The store seemed empty, with only the noxious aroma of rot drifting in from outside. Sam immediately made a mad dash for the cooler. Rows and rows of various, multi-colored drinks lined the shelves. He popped open a can of Pepsi and downed it in five quick gulps. The carbonated liquid burned his throat as it quenched his thirst. Next, he shot over to the candy aisle. Two chocolate bars quickly disappeared, followed by a bag of potato chips.

You never were smart enough to eat right, son, the dangling face of his father said.

Sam ignored it and continued searching the store.

If you're going to ignore me that's one thing, but I'll still warn you that you better beware of this store, this town, this world. A new one is coming, one where there will only be room for the dead.

His father's strange and disturbing words dug into Sam's head.

A new world? Only room for the dead? What did he mean? And how would he know? He never left home except to go to work.

Sam dropped the assorted snacks and sandwiches he'd been gathering and walked over to the front counter. He thought that if there were a phone in the place, it would be there.

The sudden thought that he'd begun to rummage through the store without asking permission, without verifying the owner was around, tapped on his conscience, so with great reluctance he felt compelled to call out to anyone who might be in the store.

"Hello? Is anybody here? I'm just getting some food and drink. I…I had a problem back at Feeter's across the road. Hello?"

The gentle creaking and groaning of the building settling in the wind was the only thing Sam heard, or at least until the white corpse suddenly stood up from behind the front counter, and brandishing a six-inch hunting knife and twisted grin, leaped over the tabletop and flung itself at him.

The stench of the thing's breath alone was enough to knock out Sam where he stood, and he found himself wondering, in those brief, suspended seconds just what had caused the man's death.

"Now I've got ya," the zombie snarled, black spittle flying from its gaping mouth.

Sam was caught off guard initially, but straightened himself upright quickly, and snatching the first thing he could get his hands on, rammed the pocket screwdriver set directly into the side of the creature's head. The zombie howled in pain and promptly crashed face down onto the counter. Thin plumes of greenish mist drifted up from its shattered head.

Sam pulled the knife from its hand, marveling at how tightly it still grasped the blade. He raised it to his eyes and admired the tool. It was a finely-honed blade, most likely tempered Swiss steel with a rippled handgrip which was molded perfectly to fit a man's hand. He waved it back and forth a few times, imitating stabbing motions, before tucking it into his back pocket.

The time he had wasted in the store suddenly occurred to Sam, so seizing whatever provisions he could find, he headed toward the door…and into the smiling, undead face of Tim Feeter.

"Hey there, Mr. Barrett," the teenage zombie sarcastically said.

His body, what was left of it, was bent every which way, causing Sam to wonder how it managed to stand up, much less move around. Sam felt his head starting to grow light again.

Was it another hallucination?

Tim lunged forward, bloodied teeth gnashing, broken fingers grasping. He managed to grab Sam, flinging him violently aside before advancing on him again on crushed legs.

Sam shook his head, trying to clear his thoughts. He was disoriented and thought he saw the same green mist floating around Tim's body that he had seen in the shop. It struck him then that he wasn't imaging it at all, that somehow, someway, the mist had something to do with what was happening.

Bout time you're using your brain for something, his father said. The face was plastered on the wall next to the cartons of cigarettes. Sam thought it ironic since his dad was somewhat of a chain- smoker his whole life; he put away two packs of Marlboros every day.

Tim was sauntering down an aisle

"We gotta speed things up a bit," he laughed as he jostled back and forth. "Don't have too much time."

But then something happened.

Sam watched open mouthed as the zombie suddenly stopped in its tracks, and without uttering another sound, turned around and started limping toward the door, not once looking back at its potential victim.

Taking advantage of the opportunity, Sam jumped to his feet and lashed out at the corpse with the knife. The blade was only six inches long but very sharp, and easily sliced into the neck of the zombie, severing its head from its body. The cranium slopped to the floor in a reeking mass, its eyes still blinking rapidly, its jaws chomping up and down.

Sam, disgusted beyond belief, landed a swift kick to the head, sending it spiraling clear out the front door of the store. It would have resembled a football shooting through.. the uprights if it weren't for the glistening entrails trailing from its stump.

"That's three points," Sam said with a smile. "That'll give me the lead."

When Sam walked out the door, what he saw not only surprised him but also sliced a clean layer of reality from everything he believed in. The sheer impossibility bordered on absurdity, but he saw it nonetheless.

Green was everywhere, covering the dirt roads and trails of Toals Creek, coating the buildings, the stores, the very foundations of the town, enveloping the heart and soul of the city in a nightmare of otherworldly color.

Sam took a cautious step onto the front porch of J.J.'s Party Store and stared in disbelief at the display. It was surreal to say the least.

"What the…"

What indeed, Son. I told you a new world is coming, one where there is only room for the dead.

Sam shook his head. "No. It can't be. It just can't be."

My advice to you is to follow your boss. It won't save you or anybody else, but at the very least you might learn something.

"Fine!" Sam shouted. "I'll do it."

Good. I knew eventually you'd do something right.

Sam wiped the pocketknife off on his pants and slipped it into his pocket. He retrieved bottled water, snacks, candy bars and cans of soda pop from the store, and started walking the way he'd seen Feeter go. He regretted that he couldn't take his Malibu, but his boss had rambled through a thicket of bushes far too dense to take a car into. And he also doubted that zombies, Feeter's or otherwise, would stick to any type of road. Whatever their purpose or destination was, he was certain that the only way he'd find any answers was to follow them, to the ends of the Earth if necessary.

Better get a move on if you're gonna catch that boss of yours. He's not gonna sit and wait for you, ya know.

*   *   *

The image of Sam's father floated about, skipping from a tree trunk here, a perched boulder there. It kept silent however, choosing to merely study its son's progress through the wilderness. Occasionally a soft grunt of satisfaction or disappointment escaped its lips.

Sam trudged onward through the brush. Following Feeter's corpse was easier than he expected it to be. Between the trail of body fluids, decayed tissue, and the smell, Sam could have tracked him blindfolded.

The tracks led north, occasionally veering to the west. Sam sat on a fallen tree stump softened by years of decay. Plates of yellow and green fungus sprouted from its sides, colors that at second glance didn't seem entirely normal. Despite the fact that he didn't know tree fungus from chocolate pudding, Sam still leaned into the growths, bringing his nose as close as he dared.

They weren't really yellow at all, only a faint hint of a dull hue bordering between light gray and something akin to a drab olive green. Sam also noticed tiny, green speckles, which upon closer inspection appeared to be growing from the fungus. A thick knot formed in his throat when he realized how closely the spots resembled the same strange greenish mist he'd seen back in town.

He immediately straightened up; his neck and lower back cracked loudly. In his peripheral vision, he then noticed the surrounding foliage. It too was generously dotted with the green spots. In fact, the more Sam looked around, the more green he saw. It decorated the trees, the ground, even a pair of large squirrels he noticed scampering by in the distance. Just how he didn't see it before he couldn't begin to guess.

It's just like I told you it would be, his father's leering image suddenly said from a dangling tree limb. *It's the new world. Only room in it for the dead...and the one who will see as a god sees.*

"What does that mean?" Sam asked angrily. "What new world? And how do you know all this?"

The face smiled grimly. It was a smile that reveled in its

73

knowledge, that rejoiced in the fact that it held information others desired.

And then the face faded into the foliage, silently becoming one with the woods.

Sam stood there, alone, frightened, and confused. His only option was clear enough (continuing to follow Feeter), but doubt began to slip into his thoughts.

What would it prove? And would he even survive?

Taking a swig of water, Sam stretched a bit and continued on his journey.

CHAPTER 14

When Deloris Bancroft pulled out onto the street, the last thing on her mind was getting into a car accident. She never even saw the oncoming truck (a mid-90's, forest- green Chevy S-10 with a cracked windshield and three bald tires). Its driver, a 17 year-old teenage boy more interested in switching worn cassettes in his second-hand radio than watching where he was driving, hadn't noticed the lady wandering into the street until he'd almost ran over her. He swerved to the left, clipping the woman's car in the process. The woman spun around from the impact as her car fell to the asphalt in a twisted heap.

The S-10 hung on two tires for a second or two before careening directly into the oncoming lane, and into the path of Deloris Bancroft's Toyota.

Deloris came to, her sight tinted by her blood and the morning sun glinting on the numerous cracks in the windshield of her car. She pushed her tangled hair out of her bruised face and sat upright. Instantly, a sharp jab of white-hot pain punched her in her gut.

Oh my God! Internal injuries!

The driver of the other car was even less lucky. His truck had spilled over onto its side. He was ejected out of the drivers' side window, leaving him unconscious and pinned under the vehicle.

He would be easy prey.

Deloris attempted to push the release button on her seatbelt, but the safety device wouldn't budge. She was held fast. She would simply have to wait for help to arrive. There was no other choice. Surely someone had to have heard the crash. Somebody must have.

The shadow descended on Deloris from behind, blotting out the warm morning sun. It moved slowly at first as if pondering the situation, as if regarding the injured person with cold, calculated indifference.

Deloris fought the urge to pass out, fully aware that releasing herself to the relative comfort of unconscious sleep would very possibly equate to a death sentence. She had to focus, she had to keep her mind alert, had to keep her blood pumping.

The shadow stepped forward, temporarily covering Deloris in cool shade. The stench of the person wafted up her nose, stinging her already damaged senses with its aroma of death and decay.

And then, seconds before her short life ended, Deloris noticed one peculiar aspect about her killer: the person was missing their left hand.

*   *   *

Jerry watched the horrible scenario unfold from his hiding spot. The sub-compact car hardly provided adequate protection from being seen by his wife, but it worked nonetheless. He found himself wondering just why Stephanie had taken the time to attack others but had left him untouched earlier in their home. Could it be that she still harbored some type of feeling for him? Could there still be some traces of humanity left in her body?

A tear welled in Jerry's eye and fell to the curb. He still felt bad for the poor woman in the car. If only he could have warned her somehow; it might have saved her life. In a way he felt responsible somehow. Stephanie was his wife after all.

But it wasn't meant to be. She would have died anyway, and the kid probably would have too; the accident wasn't a pretty sight.

Stephanie stopped her grisly feast and stood up, a thick chunk of yellowed body fat streaked with watery red glistening in her mouth. She dropped the body of the dead woman to the ground and abruptly walked away, never once looking back. It was as if she simply wasn't hungry any more.

Jerry watched in confusion as his dead wife meandered away from the car wrecks and stumbled straight into the surrounding woods, a sickening trail of blood in her wake. Her expression was one of grim satisfaction mixed with equal parts annoyance and resignation.

"What happened?" the young man asked from behind Jerry. His eyes were wild with fear and panic. "Is anyone hurt? We have to see if anyone is injured."

Jerry was not only startled by the kid practically appearing out of nowhere, but also annoyed. The kid's breath stank like an open dumpster.

"Slow down there, Son," he said, trying to keep his voice down. "There's no sense in worrying about those poor people. They're already dead."

"You got that right," came the unexpected reply.

And with those cryptic words Jerry smelled the other aroma coming from the kid. It was the stench of rot. He slowly turned around.

"Name's Feeter. Tim Feeter," the dangling head said with the calmness of someone talking about a baseball game or the weather.

The corpse was proudly displaying its own head, holding it up at eye level to Jerry. The open wound that had been its neck was trickling a nauseating substance composed of blood, liquefying tissue, and strange green droplets.

Jerry swung around quickly, knocking the zombie's twisted legs out from under it. Tim dropped his head, a surprised look spread across its face. He went down hard, smashing into the ground with enough force to knock the wind out of a living person.

But he wasn't alive.

With deadly accuracy, Tim reared back up into a sitting position; his mutilated head lain grotesquely next to his body. Its eyes were blinking open and shut rapidly, its mouth gibbering in frothy rage. He swung his arms around in a rapid motion, narrowly missing Jerry's face.

Jerry sprang to his feet. Shaking off a momentary flash of disorientation, he landed a solid hit squarely between the head's eyes with his foot, sending the thing clear across the street. He watched it in disbelieving satisfaction as it sailed high into the air, skirting several trees in the process, before landing in a row of shrubbery over fifty feet away.

The zombie's headless body rolled over onto its side. Its legs were so mangled and twisted it could hardly stand up. It reminded Jerry, in an odd sort of way, of a turtle flipped over onto its back. He used to capture turtles in Anwer's Pond when he was a kid. But he didn't want to catch this particular turtle. He'd just as soon let it wallow in its frustrated misery.

"Nice to meet you, Tim," he sarcastically quipped. "Now if you'll excuse me I have to track down my wife."

The zombie's body tried vainly to right itself, clawing at the air, squirming like a sliced in half worm on a rain-soaked sidewalk. Green fungus leaked from the stump where its head used to be, puddling in thick pools on the curb. It strained every way a human body could twist and turn, and some a human was never meant to.

Jerry looked down at the pathetic display. His heart felt a slight trace of pity for the creature, but he set it aside. In life he was sure Tim Feeter was probably a nice kid; he had probably enjoyed fishing, looking at girls, hanging out with friends, or doing whatever kids did nowadays. But that was then and this was now, and that same kid had tried to kill him.

With an indifferent smirk, Jerry landed a swift, violent kick into the ribs of the body. The bones cracked from the blow, each sound bolstering his confidence that he just might be able to save the day after all. He then darted off past the wrecked cars and motionless bodies. He had to follow Stephanie.

*　　　　　*　　　　　*

The woods were dense, letting only a few sparse rays of sunlight through the leaves. A stiff wind was gradually picking up, gently bending and swaying the trees and bushes to its whim.

Jerry winced when he realized he was downwind from the breeze. The stench of death was drifting right into his face, turning his stomach and making his eyes water.

But it was from Stephanie, he thought with a smile. *It's from her. The smell, the blood, the bits and pieces of her body. They're all from her.*

The irrationality of his thoughts suddenly struck him. Here he was, a man, a father, a husband, chasing the remaining shreds of his family, dodging the undead, spiraling toward a destination that he knew nothing about. The mere idea froze the blood in his veins. What if

Stephanie attacked him again? Would he be able to fend her off? And would he be able deal with it again? Could he handle the pain?

The tears started then, leaking from his eyes, dribbling down his cheeks. They sapped his strength, a common effect that they had on most men. It simply wasn't masculine to show one's true feelings. No matter what women said, they still wanted, and expected, men to stay strong and be tough.

Continuing on, Jerry plodded through the thick foliage, climbing over rotted tree stumps, stepping around embedded boulders and dangling branches. He had to reach deep inside himself for strength. He really wanted to see Stephanie again, no matter what condition she was in. He just needed to see her face one more time. There were too many memories to simply shut out and leave alone. It just wasn't in him to do that.

The lone figure appeared in his peripheral vision off to the left, dragging him away from his thoughts. The person was a man, short, somewhat portly, and dressed in a tattered gray business suit. Dark stains spotted his clothes as he shambled along in a slow gait. Occasionally a low hanging tree branch or stone would temporarily impede his movements. Despite his distance, Jerry could see the man wasn't alive.

He was, however, going in the same direction.

Who was this man? Where had he come from? Highland Hills was to the east, and this man was obviously heading north. The man's steps were erratic, but still suggested he had a definite destination in mind. There was a purpose in his stride.

Jerry wanted to call out to the man but thought better of it. He was a zombie, and although he probably wouldn't have paid too much attention to him, Jerry still didn't want to take any chances. Instead, he tucked his gun back into his pocket and crouched down in the brush to scout the immediate area.

The man continued on his way, either oblivious to, or not caring who saw him. Jerry watched him from behind a gnarled tree, doing his best to ignore the buzzing flies around his head. He suspected the zombie man wasn't bothered too much by the insects.

There was something strangely familiar about him. Jerry couldn't put his finger on it, but it was there. The way he walked, his mannerisms, his clothes, they were all familiar somehow.

The zombie eventually sensed it was being watched. In its rudimentary brain it could feel the gaze of another. It sniffed the forest air momentarily, cocking its rotting head to one side and then the other. It smelled a living human being.

Jerry froze on the spot when the zombie swung a baleful stare directly at him.

"I told you, Mr. Ott, that I want that Bearings Proposal on my desk!"

Mr. Tompsett? It was Mr. Tompsett!

Fondling the trigger on his pistol, Jerry stood up and confronted his dead boss.

"Yeah, it's me. Mr. Tompsett," he replied in a nervous voice. His knees were shaking. "And you better stay right where you are. I'm armed."

Mr. Tompsett let a crooked smile escape. His desiccated lips split wide open revealing a mostly toothless maw. Slick, bloody drool dribbled down the front of his soiled suit. His blank eyes widened. His dangling hands tightened into fists.

And then without another sound he turned away, leaving his stench and many unanswered questions behind.

Jerry decided to follow his dead boss. Despite all he'd seen, he still found himself reveling in the fact that he wouldn't have to jump to Tompsett's beck and call anymore. The hell with the Bearings Proposal, and Tompsett's afternoon meetings that frequently ran past five o'clock, and the stupid little cubicle that was barely big enough to house his desk or computer. All of it could simply drop into the ocean as far as he was concerned. It could disappear in a giant wisp of smoke.

The zombie was moving along slowly. Jerry could see it walked with great reluctance, as if it were being forced to travel, pulled along unwillingly to an unknown destination. But what was forcing it?

Jerry suppressed the constant urge to give up. He'd been through a lot. He was tired. He was dirty. But above all he was scared.

He was scared of not being able to find Martin. He was scared of having to tell his remaining son that his mother was dead. That his brother and sister were dead. He was scared of what he might find by following Stephanie or Tompsett. And he was scared of how he would deal with all of this. Would his mind be able to accept what was happening? A man's mind is preset, programmed to only comprehend so much. What is real? What is possible? Imagination is a useful tool to expand those limitations, but it dwells in the mind alone. And when the mind is confronted, physically confronted by the impossible, by something that just can't possibly be but is, it tries desperately to wrap itself around that impossibility. It tries to understand it, to label it with rationality, with common sense. But it doesn't always succeed. And when that happens, the mind will try to hide.

Jerry stayed approximately fifty feet behind Tompsett; close enough to keep an eye on him, but far enough away that if he suddenly turned and decided he was hungry, Jerry would have enough time to react.

The other figure came into Jerry's view off to his right. The slow waddle and disoriented stature gave it away as a zombie. Its gait was unmistakable. It moved in studded steps, stumbling over rocks and humps of dirt and leaves. It was smaller than Tompsett, possibly a female.

Treading softly on the desiccated leaves beneath his feet, Jerry held his breath. He didn't want to give himself away. *Double Q* needed to be used again. Quick and quiet, although the second aspect needed to be implemented with much more force. Stealth was the order of the day.

The second zombie was apparently moving in the same direction as Tompsett, running at about a forty-five degree angle before gradually assuming a parallel course. Jerry watched the two. He slipped a dented water bottle out of his bag and took a nervous sip, spilling more than he drank. Looking around, Jerry noticed the faint, but obvious reflections of a greenish tint. The shade differed from the natural fresh green from Mother Nature's palette. It was luminescent somehow, almost radiant, and yet simultaneously dull and faded. It was an unnatural concoction of impossible hues.

Slipping the water bottle back into his bag, Jerry watched the zombies suddenly halt in their tracks. The smaller one then turned to face him. With a knot in his stomach, Jerry finally recognized the dead person. The missing left hand was a dead giveaway.

CHAPTER 15

Al Moser swung lazily on the front porch swing of his modest, but comfortable, ranch-style house. His mind roamed between his long past glories in World War II (he was a decorated officer who once captured an entire platoon of enemy soldiers) and the somber memories of the love he had lost to a horrific car crash (which he still blamed himself for causing).

In the eighty two years he lived through, he'd seen a lot. He witnessed the Civil Rights movement firsthand. He watched Kennedy get his head blown off on that November day back in '63. He'd seen man take his first step on the moon and he'd seen the invention of television, computers, and cell phones. He endured a bout with malaria, the loss of a finger, and the reign of several presidents, both Democrat and Republican; all just politicians in the end.

Watching a lone blue jay glide by overhead, Al wished he could still hear them. Since losing his hearing a decade earlier (the end result of a bad virus which he neglected to have tested), he'd almost grown appreciative of his handicap.

Almost.

True, sometimes it allowed him to experience an inner peace of sorts, but if given the choice, he most certainly would want to have it back.

He observed the bird in its own personal domain, wishing all the while he could hear it chirping away, or making whatever sounds birds made. Without sound, the bird seemed to be nothing more than a soaring dot, veering upwards higher and higher as it ventured along on its journey.

Al's silent world then suddenly had a visitor, one who the deaf old man obviously did not hear, or unfortunately for him…see.

Mrs. Geraldine Baxter, the new grandmother, the avid reader, the recently re-animated corpse who had died of a sudden brain aneurism, came shuffling out the front door of Abby Convalescent Home.

She instantly focused her dead gaze and gore-stained hunger on the lone occupant of the porch: one Mr. Albert Moser, veteran of World War II. With one vicious arc of her arm, she efficiently separated most of Mr. Moser's face from his head. Eyeballs, dentures, and a bulbous nose disintegrated   against the concrete porch slab. Bits of aged brain matter and blood-soaked flesh splashed across Mrs. Baxter. Al Moser never heard, or felt, a thing.

Mrs. Baxter looked down at the body of the dead man slumped over in its rocking chair. Normally it would have rung the dinner bell for her, and she did contemplate gorging herself on the remains for a brief second or two, but she couldn't do it.

With a hollow sigh of resignation, she stepped past the bloody carcass and out into the streets of Highland Hills.

*   *   *

Grady Preston pinched his nose as he tiptoed across the porch. The blood, the smell, the very idea that just a short time ago the mass of reeking gore on the
porch had been a living, breathing, human being tapped on his conscience. But he justified it to himself with a quick thought.

"Just another stepping stone to the special spot," he giggled. "Just another arrow on the map, and maps are meant to be followed."

He sauntered out onto the road, marveling at how such carnage could occur in such a short time. He was surprised that no police officers had arrived yet, but fully expected them to at any minute. Hastily scooting away from his prison, he pulled his afghan up over his scrawny shoulders. Even though it was a reasonably pleasant day, his circulation wasn't what it used to be. Behind him he could hear frantic people scuttling back and forth, screaming in fear and pain, crying in anguish, moaning in horrified disbelief. Mrs. Baxter had apparently done a fine job. The place was a mess.

Grady smiled a little bit wider. Everything was going perfectly. He had been told there would be a special spot where mankind's new horizon would germinate, but not told where the location was. He had a strong hunch it would be north, and since the only other town within a stone's throw was Toals Creek off to the west, he surmised that the area must be in a heavily wooded location, perhaps near the San Basin River. But regardless, Grady knew he must follow the trail Mrs. Baxter had laid out before him.

He decided to discard his afghan, and with it any residual ties to his former life. He could only hope that Grace would forgive him. "Just like a road map," he said to himself while looking out at the woods. "All I have to do is follow the trail." And then he plodded across the street, and started on the bloody trail left by Mrs. Baxter in front of him.

*   *   *

Cliff was watching the old man from the window of room C-7. He'd been delivering reading materials to the rooms when all the commotion had started. After ducking underneath a bed, he managed to just catch a glimpse of Mrs. Baxter waddling past the doorway. She was streaked with gore and judging by the screams, Cliff knew something unnatural and dangerous was happening. He eventually worked up enough courage to venture from his hiding spot.

"What happened!" he shouted at Vic (the afternoon janitor) who was running for his life like everyone else.

"I... I don't know! Some old lady came back from the dead and started attacking people! She killed some of them too!"

Cliff had always liked Vic. He was an honest guy, friendly and outgoing to a fault, and would give you the shirt off of his back. But Cliff found himself doubting the young janitor.

But then the recollection of what he'd seen (or thought he saw) with the old man, Mr. Grady Preston, in C-3 dropped into this mind and took root there, validating the possibility of what Vic claimed.

"Are you sure?"

"Man, I don't know. All I do know is I'm getting outta here man. I quit!"

Cliff felt bad for Vic. He really did. He was a good man who, when confronted with a nightmare, chose to turn tail and run. Cliff wondered to himself why he wasn't doing the same thing.

Cliff stood there, watching the other people scrambling around like field mice. The same people he worked with and helped care for.

There was Mr. Sather from room B-9, his snow-white hair whipping around his small head; Tina, the single mother who worked part-time in the Home. Cliff had thought of asking her out once or twice but didn't want the extra baggage of two small kids. It would have been a package deal, and he just wasn't ready to commit to something like that. And Caroline Sudt, a quiet, middle-aged woman who kept to herself so much that Cliff only recently learned her last name despite working with her for quite some time.

And there were others also: his supervisor Mr. Frol, a strict, thoroughly methodical man who never wanted to hear excuses, regardless of their validity. And Lori, an intelligent God-fearing woman who was always smiling and loved animals. She worked in the front office with Jane, and the two never seemed to get along with each other. And Connie, and Zach and Mr. Inser, and many others all running for their very lives down the cluttered corridor, bumping into each other, falling against walls, knocking over carts trying to get away any way they could.

Cliff recognized most of them in one way or another. He felt like grabbing each and every one of them by the shoulders and shaking some sense into them. Everyone that is except for Mr. Frol. Cliff mused to himself that he could go on his way.

The front door offered little in the way of escape, unless of course one was willing to navigate through the remains of Mr. Moser. That fact caused the residents, visitors, and employees to bottleneck in the hallway. Within a few minutes, the passageway was a throbbing mass of bodies, some bloodied, some unharmed, but all frantic to escape.

When he saw the chaos in the hallway Cliff slid to a stop. Looking for another way out, he quickly decided on trying for the rear delivery door. Simmons, Benny, Allison, and Mrs. Cooper received supplies through that same door nearly every day, stocking the Home with the various food and equipment needed for daily operations.

The dining room was dimly lit, the light aroma of past meals and discarded food hung in the air. Cliff sniffed the odor. His stomach grumbled. He hadn't eaten since that morning. But there was another dimension to the smell. At first, Cliff thought it was one of rot and decay; the sour odor made him crinkle his nose. But there was something else as well, an earthly smell reminiscent of walking through the woods after a heavy rain.

Taking cautious steps, Cliff weaved his way through the numerous plastic chairs and folding tables. He couldn't see too well but knew the room good enough to avoid most obstacles.

The dim light masked most of the fungus-like growth throughout the room. A thin, green film was spread out evenly over the polished tile floor and clung to table and chair legs, countertops, and even the light fixtures.

His mind raced with attempts to fasten logical explanations to the nightmare. Cliff reeled from the implications. People had been killed. The dead walked. And the strange old man in C-3, Grady Preston. It all weighed heavily on his mind.

The guttural moan coming from the back stockroom froze his thoughts immediately. He took a step forward, then another.

"Hello? Who's there? I'm armed."

His words were hollow and were backed with little confidence. All was silent except for an oversized wall clock ticking away the seconds of the day. A dark atmosphere clung to the room, choking any semblance of normalcy. Cliff debated on continuing to work his way back to the stockroom door; it could very well prove to be the only safe exit from the building, but he didn't know what might be waiting for him. Turning around was a tempting option as well.

The dark figure of Mrs. Cooper loomed up from the shadows. She swayed not more than twenty feet in front of where Cliff stood. A low, raspy mumbling dribbled from her half closed mouth. Her large head swung from side to side.

"Mrs. Cooper? Is that you?" Cliff asked, despite knowing perfectly well who it was. "I'm just trying to find a way out of here. There have been some people killed. We need to evacuate."

No response. The clock continued to tick away the time.

Wishing he had a flashlight, Cliff turned abruptly and made a beeline for the dimmer switches on the far wall. He missed them when he first entered the room, summing it up to an irrational thought that there would be no power. A part of him really didn't want to see Mrs. Cooper, but his survival might depend on it. She was blocking the way to the back room, and going through her might be his only option.

The figure lurched forward, shambling along surprisingly quickly for such a large person. Within a few seconds, Mrs. Cooper was right in front of Cliff, her cold hands reaching out eagerly for him just as he slid the dimmer switches up to full.

The first thing Cliff noticed was green. A lightly translucent shade of the color coated everything in sight in the room. The floor was alive with spongy, bulbous, mushroom-like growths.

The zombie was on him in an instant.

Bloody teeth gnashed at his neck as the room flooded with light. The grip was immensely strong. Cliff yelped in pain as he tried to dislodge the corpse from his body. Cracked fingernails bore into his shoulders, drawing blood and leaving painful welts. Fetid breath fogged his senses.

"What the…Mrs. Cooper? What are you doing?"

"Just want to make sure you don't leave the lights on, Dear." The voice was dry, void of life, completely lacking any warmth or soul. "It's the new world. It's coming. Death will consume life." The face was gaunt and wrinkled, pressing up against Cliff's. It spoke clearly however; the watery eyes conveyed its terrible message perfectly.

Cliff pushed away from the thing. He managed to orient himself, standing upright to face his antagonist. The face was one he recognized; he'd seen it many times at the Home. But now it was a face of evil, dark hunger tainted its visage.

"Get away from me. I'll…I'll…"

"You'll what? Be dinner?"

The corpse continued advancing. Behind it two more figures emerged, flanking Mrs. Cooper's body: Allison Bathn and Benny Yourt. They were also employees at the Home. And now both were dead, and along with Mrs. Cooper, were wading through the fungus toward Cliff.

Cliff stumbled backwards, falling into the hallway, trying desperately to crawl away from the dead. He cringed when he felt the spongy texture of the floor on his hands. It covered his palms; the thick green growth was everywhere.

The three corpses were grinning from rotten ear to rotten ear. Benny and Allison had chunks of their arms and necks chewed off; no doubt Mrs. Cooper had been the first one to die and had caused their deaths.

Getting up on his feet, Cliff immediately sprinted down the hallway. Behind him he could hear the zombies taunting him.

"Leaving so soon? We're just getting started." The words of the dead sustained a chilling conviction of sarcasm.

The front door of the Home was directly in front of Cliff. It was framed with unnatural green growth but still seemed to be intact. Cliff resisted looking back as he ran for the door. The two bodies in the hallway were stirring with life, and one of them reached for him as he passed by it. The cold fingers narrowly missed his ankle.

And just as he reached the front door, a lone figure appeared in the doorway. It was a woman, an elderly woman who wore a tattered dress from another era along with a friendly smile. Cliff ground to a sudden halt. He momentarily lost himself in the woman's eyes. There was a certain magnetism in them.

"Pardon me young man," the woman said quietly, "but I believe that this is Abby Convalescent Home if I'm not mistaken. Is that right? Am I in the correct place?"

Cliff struggled for a reply.

The woman smiled even wider; her glassy eyes narrowed.

"I'm here to see someone. My husband. A Mr. Grady Preston."

Cliff's heart skipped a beat.

"You see, I'm his wife. My name is Grace."

CHAPTER 16

The mosquitoes buzzed around Ryan's head. The trail left by Wade was becoming harder and harder to follow; damp twigs and leaves obscured any chance of footprints, and the breeze at his back was making it difficult to follow any type of scent. A tint of unnatural green was glazed across the landscape.

Looking around, Ryan figured he traveled about a mile, maybe two. The sun was peeking through the trees, but only enough to create numerous shadows on the ground. The trees were dense, and Ryan had to literally push his way along through them. But he knew he was on the right path because he found bits and pieces of his zombie neighbor that either fell off the body or were snagged on a branch or rock as the creature shambled along.

"Never thought I'd miss Highland Hills," he joked to nobody but himself. The mere sound of a voice, even his own, helped to relieve some of the tension. He felt like a rubber band stretched taut, ready to snap at any moment.

"Well, at least I'm getting some exercise and fresh air," he mumbled. "Only wish I had my bike. But of course it'd been tough through all this growth."

Ryan stopped in his tracks; his words fell to the ground. A sixth sense warned him someone was approaching. He gripped the baseball bat in his sweaty hands. The figure appeared from behind a huge tree. First a head, deformed by decay, and then a set of hands which quickly curled into threatening fists. Ryan readied his bat as if he were standing at home plate. He'd dealt with zombies before, he could do it again. He steeled his nerves to face the threat head on.

The zombie was grinning and frowning simultaneously and appeared to Ryan to be wrestling with its own thoughts. It wanted to attack, to assuage its hunger, the pain in its cramped gut, but something was prohibiting it from doing so.

Slowly, Ryan approached the corpse. If it wasn't going to come to him, he would go to it. The thought of following it instead of his neighbor did float through his mind, and he gave it some thought. What if he couldn't find Wade? After all, one zombie was as good as another for tracking, wasn't it? What difference would it really make?

Ryan then saw the flash directly behind the zombie's head. It lasted only a fraction of a second, but he knew what it was almost immediately.

The corpse of Old Man Feeter crumbled to the ground, the back of its head splayed wide open like a blood-filled piñata. It fell face first into a pile of damp, fungus- covered tree branches and leaves.

Ryan stared wide-eyed at the unkempt man who had wielded the deadly branch like a club. The man's eyes were wild with grim satisfaction.

"Howdy," Sam called out. "I've wanted to do that for a very long time."

Ryan felt both angry and relieved. He wouldn't have to face the zombie, but now he didn't have one to follow either.

"Thanks, I guess," he blurted out. "But I needed one of those...those things to follow."

"I was following that one," Sam replied with a grin. "He was my boss; couldn't stand that guy. He killed his own son, ya know."

Ryan cringed. "Yeah, after what I've seen I believe it."

"Sam. Sam Barrett. I'm from Toals Creek." He offered a grimy hand.

Ryan shook it. "Ryan Connelly. I'm from Highland Hills."

"We're practically neighbors then."

"Yeah, I guess in a way we are."

Sam sat down on a large rock. He ignored the pressing face of his father in the trees.

A new world. Only room for the...

"So what are you doing way out here?"

Ryan sat across from Sam, resting his baseball bat across his knees. "Well, I guess I'm doing the same thing as you are: following one of those things to see where it's going. Course I don't exactly know just why I'm following it."

Sam laughed out loud. "Yeah, me too. I started out trying to see where my boss was heading, but got sick and tired of trailing his dead butt through these woods."

The two men sat opposite each other; an uneasy aura of nervousness and weariness settled between them. The woods were silent by then, except for the occasional bird chirping overhead or squirrel scampering along the ground. They shared water and food and sparse conversation. Each had endured impossible horrors and was trying to make sense of it. This common goal bound them together, and they both knew it.

CHAPTER 17

Louise Sampson cowered in the corner of her finished basement. The space had been her and her husband's pride and joy. Her husband Rick and their son Jack had fixed it up over the course of the last two years, and the whole family loved spending time in it. There was a forty-two-inch plasma television mounted next to the carved mahogany bar. Custom oak paneling stretched across the walls. Occasionally, a tasteful painting hung on the wall. And it was all topped off by a dropped ceiling with specially ordered tinted tiles and recessed fluorescent lighting. Cream colored office carpet covered the floor.

But now the room that Louise and her family had enjoyed so much had turned into something of a prison.

"We know you're down there, Honey," Rick snorted from behind the upstairs door. It was the only barrier between them. "Me and Jack are here."

"Hi, Mom."

Louise shuddered. She knew her husband and son were dead. She saw the bodies. She also saw the other person in her home, the man who had attacked her family. The man covered in the strange green substance. The man who was already dead when he pushed his way through their front door and into their living room.

The door at the top of the stairs was splintering badly. The two zombies were pummeling it with kitchen knives, Louise's kitchen knives. The wood buckled beneath the assault. Rick's work boots, the same ones Louise had literally forced him to buy (he needed them so much for work, but was worried about the cost), slammed into the door again and again.

"Come on, Honey. We wanna spend time in the basement."

Louise looked around the room. The amenities that in the past had offered so much pleasure, so much enjoyment, now seemed to only promise painful memories of what once was but would never be again.

Highland Hills was to be their paradise. They moved there to get away from the grind and pollution of the big city. Rick was going to start a small woodworking business in the near future, and Jack, when he was between girlfriends, was finishing up his junior year in high school. He had plans to attend college to study chemistry, preferably on campus.

The only remaining barrier between Louise and certain death finally collapsed. Chunks of splintered wood cascaded down the staircase, and the polished aluminum hinges and door handle clanked to the foot of the stairs. Green mist preceded the two zombies down the stairs and quickly spread across the basement. Louise huddled tighter and tighter in the far corner of the small space next to the wet bar.

Alcohol is flammable, she thought. She'd seen it in the movies. The hero would stuff a piece of cloth into a bottle of liquor and light the end of it. Then all you had to do was toss the bottle and it would explode into a blazing fireball, spreading flames as far as the liquid spilt. Crude, but effective.

Louise struggled to her feet and yanked a bottle of whiskey from the mirrored wall behind the bar.

"I hope this is a good year," she half-joked to herself.

Tearing off a strip of her blouse, she then unscrewed the cap on the bottle and pushed the fabric into the opening. A quick shake of the bottle soaked the cloth, producing the desired effect. Just like that, the bottle had been transformed from a necessity at any bar into a formidable weapon.

The cold stench drifted into her face.

"Hi, Mom," the teenage zombie sneered. "You forgot you'd still need this."

Louise's heart sank into her stomach when her son, her dead son, held up a small, stainless steel lighter; a thin, yellow flame danced at the tip.

The screams only lasted for a brief moment, perhaps two, and then abruptly were cut off.

Minutes later, the dead family, complete once again, scrambled up the staircase and out the front door of the house, joining the dozens of other walking dead in the streets of Highland Hills.

Jerry felt like throwing caution to the wind and running to Stephanie. He wanted nothing else but to embrace her, to forget all that she'd done, all that had happened to him, but the thought of Martin nudged him away from the suicidal notion. That and the memory of Stephanie's dead grin, complete with cracked teeth and split gray flesh.

The zombies continued waddling along through the woods. Occasionally one would trip over a branch or rock, crash into the ground, and quickly get back up again, oblivious to its injuries. Jerry kept his distance from them, trying to stay concealed behind trees, attempting to avoid touching anything; the strange green fungus was everywhere. But something told him he didn't need to hide like he was. The zombies didn't seem to care that he was following them. They merely stumbled along on their mysterious quest, shambling toward a destination most likely as much of a mystery to them as it was to Jerry.

The shadow caught Jerry's eye in mid-thought. It was small (possibly a scavenger of some sort) and darted between waist- high brush and moss-covered boulders. It was quick, silent, and fluid in its movements. He slipped his gun out from his pocket and feathered the trigger. He didn't want to draw attention to himself, but he realized that he might not have a choice in the matter.

Another shadow skirted a row of pine trees. There were two of them; Jerry was sure of it. His gun's barrel rested in his left palm, ready for action if need be.

And then he saw one of them, and much to his surprise and relief, it wasn't a zombie.

The man was young, probably no more than twenty-five, maybe thirty, and he wielded a black baseball bat. The man then noticed Jerry and motioned for the other figure to join him against a large tree trunk. Both of the men looked at Jerry. One of them waved.

Jerry lowered his gun and waved back. The two men scuttled over to where he was hiding, and settling in, introduced themselves.

"I'm Ryan. Ryan Connelly from Highland Hills. This is Sam

from Toals Creek.

" I'm Jerry. Jerry Ott. I'm also from Highland Hills."

Ryan's face brightened "Really? What part?"

"Northern burbs by Palmer Blvd."

"No kidding!" Ryan exclaimed. "I'm near there too, just past the development site on Sempter and Cross."

Jerry smiled. "My oldest worked there before he left for college."

"Small world."

"Yeah. It sure is sometimes."

Sam had been alternating between watching Jerry and Ryan and the movement of the zombies. His head was swimming on his shoulders; he'd never gone this long without his medication. He slipped between reality and illusion, sometimes having trouble differentiating between the two.

And then he saw them. There were dozens and dozens of them, and they came from all directions.

"Uhh guys," he moaned, tapping Ryan on the shoulders. "I really hate to break up your friendly little conversation, but I think we have some company."

Both Jerry and Ryan stopped talking and looked over to where Sam was pointing. Their blood froze in their veins.

The zombies were too numerous to count. Hordes of the undead monsters in varying stages of decay meandered through the woods, bumping into each other, groaning in aimless distress. They were slaves to an unknown force beyond their power to resist. A distorted sense of resignation shone on each of their pallid faces.

"Where did they all come from?" Ryan whispered. His bat was held painfully tight in his hands. His knuckles were white.

Jerry stared in disbelief. Stephanie was still there, walking slowly alongside many other zombies, and for this small token he was grateful. He still allowed a small flame to burn in his heart for her. He was still in love with his wife and the mother of his children, and all the memories he had of her (for better or worse) were there, although diluted by the situation and her present condition.

Almost as if she heard him, Stephanie briefly paused from her journey. She twisted her head around and locked her dead gaze directly on her husband. Jerry looked back. And for a moment, for just a brief moment in time, there was a bond of love in that gaze, however small and faint.

"Jerry? Jerry!" Sam tapped Jerry on the back. He'd seen the unnatural connection between him and the woman zombie, and it made him sick.

Jerry snapped out of it and immediately looked away.

"So where you guys think they're heading?" Ryan asked. A sudden image of his black beauty Louisville bat opening up the zombie's heads flashed through his mind. He smiled.

Sam was twisting the blade of his knife into the ground. He looked down. His father's face glared up at him, the steel blade buried between his eyes.

A new world, son. Only room for the...

Sam pushed the knife further into the face, choking off the words.

"Don't want to hear it now Dad," he grunted. "Not now."

Both Ryan and Jerry looked at their new friend. Concern spread across their faces.

"You all right there?" Jerry asked. His eyes alternated between Sam and Stephanie.

Sam forced a smile. "Sorry, guys. Don't worry about me; I'm fine."

Jerry smiled. "Good. So where do you guys think they're going?"

"Well, one thing is for sure," Ryan replied, "they're all heading in the same direction."

"We gonna wait here forever or are we gonna follow them?" Sam chimed in. Jerry felt annoyed. "Take it easy there, Sam. We've all been through a lot. What we need now is patience. Going in half-cocked could be suicide."

"He's right," Ryan added. "I really don't want to run into my neighbor again unless I'm really ready for it. Need to know what were up against."

Jerry nodded in approval.

The smell drifted into their faces, knotting up their stomachs with nausea. The three men froze, too afraid and too stunned to react. A lone figure approached.

"So hungry," the female zombie wailed. "So hungry, but can't feed. Can't feed."

Jerry recognized the voice. He'd heard it many times before when he dropped Wendy off at her dance class.

The ragged corpse of Ms. Teamont wallowed in the damp brush. She sensed living, breathing people nearby, so close she could smell them. For a second, a rush of excitement overcame her bloodless face. Frayed black hair dangled over her small shoulders. A bloated, gray tongue lolled past thin, pale lips. Skeletal hands clenched and stretched.

"I can smell you," she growled in the same voice Jerry remembered so well. All he had to do was close his eyes and he would be transported back to the dance class. His little girl would be there as well; her braided hair and sparkling eyes spawned pride in her father.

The frail woman corpse shifted from its left to its right, affording it a clearer view of the three men huddling beside a fallen tree. She gazed down at them with clouded eyes.

"I see you now," it said. Jerry winced in disgust as droplets of green goo dripped off of its tongue as it spoke. "And Mr. Ott, how good to see you again."

Jerry almost responded to the creature, but stopped himself. He gripped his gun tighter and tighter. His finger rested on the trigger.

Ms. Teamont's emancipated face split into an evil grin. The men looked up at the zombie and readied their meager weapons: a small, single-caliber handgun, a hunting knife, a Louisville black beauty baseball bat.

"We'll get you eventually," the corpse warned. "A new world is coming and you," she pointed a bony finger at the men, "will all be a part of it...literally."

And with those cryptic words, the corpse of Ms. Teamont,

dance instructor at Highland Hills Dance Studio, shuffled away, joining the other dead on their mysterious journey through the woods.

CHAPTER 18

The sun peeked through the treetops on its daily trip across the blue sky. The temperature hovered steadily near sixty-five degrees, although the forecast for the day promised highs in the mid to upper eighties.

Cliff lazily lifted his eyelids and immediately squinted from the bright rays of morning sunshine streaming into his bedroom. Above him, fastened securely to the ceiling, was a huge, three foot by five-foot poster of his favorite rock band (Rush). The talented trio's rock star faces stared down at him.

"Morning Geddy, Alex, Neil. Hope you guys have been working hard on that new album. Can't wait to hear it. Hopefully it'll be as good as 2112."

The rock stars didn't reply.

Cliff rolled out of his bed and stretched to the ceiling, grimacing in satisfaction at the numerous pops and cracks his spine made as it adjusted. The day's possibilities swam through his head: hang out at Galaxy Arcade on Gratiot Avenue? He could get a hold of a couple of his buddies, Mark Waffe, Gary Warrick, Tom Lauren, and hook up to rifle through ten bucks worth of quarters playing Space Invaders, Q-bert, and Dragon's Lair. He still held the record for Stargate, the by-product of Space Invaders which was just as much fun. He topped two million in points twice.

Another possible way to spend the day would be to help his dad work on the 1970 Mustang. Bright red and packing a lean 351 Cleveland motor with a Carter four-barrel carburetor, it looked as good as it ran. He always joked that if he had a dollar for every compliment he got on it he'd be a millionaire many times over.

And there were other things to do as well. He could pull out his bike and take a trip out to the lakes (Higgens and Houghton), or see about setting up a ballgame at Ridgewood Elementary, or see what was playing at Cinemark 16 near Universal Mall. Or maybe he could …

Cliff sat alone in his bedroom, slumped forward and wishing the thoughts, images, and the dreams wouldn't drift away. But they did.

Inevitably, every single aspect of the time period he was reliving through his memories gradually slipped from his perceived reality back into the reality of the present. And then, they all vanished under the weight of his current situation. 1982 was drifting away.

"Young man? Are you listening to me? Hello?"

Cliff stood there, still at the front door of Abby Convalescent Home, still in Highland Hills, neighboring, middle-of-nowhere town to Toals Creek, another middle-of-nowhere town, still bearing the scars, both mental and physical, of the rampaging zombies. His stomach churned.

"Oh, I...I'm sorry," he mumbled. "I just..."

"That's all right, Young Man," Grace replied through a soft, grandmotherly smile. "I understand. From what I gather, quite a bit has transpired here recently." She turned and faced the road, occasionally glancing down at the bloody trails leading away from the front porch. "Unfortunately, it is all as I expected. This moment in time has been perched upon the edge of my conscience for a long time, years, perhaps for decades."

The odd way the woman talked puzzled Cliff, but he found himself becoming lost in her words nonetheless.

A sudden realization gripped his mind then. *The zombies! The walking dead! Where did they go?*

"Calm yourself," the woman said with a wink. "You needn't worry yourself about them right now. I believe that most of the ones from this building have already left."

Cliff nodded. A wave of relief washed over him. He was comforted by the woman's words but distressed by the fact that she had apparently read his thoughts.

"You see, my husband was placed in this establishment many years ago by me." Her face grew long with remorse. "At first, we were happy. We fed off of each other's love, and desired to spend much time together. I was a stranger here and my husband helped me integrate my beliefs, and my culture into my new home. In short, Mister..."

"Cliff. Cliff Roaper."

"Cliff. He reassured me."

"You sound as if you're from another planet or something."

Grace turned around and faced Cliff. Her features transformed from warm and friendly to deathly serious. Her eyes narrowed. "Different planets, different star systems, different dimensions, it is all the same. Only the perception of the individual creates any differences between them."

"I'm afraid I don't understand."

"Suffice it to say that I am not from this place. But we have spent too much time here already. We must move away from here and discover the whereabouts of my husband."

Cliff nodded. If he wouldn't have seen some of the stuff he'd seen recently, he would've thought that Grace Preston or Klaato or ET, or whatever her name was, was certifiably insane.

"You lead the way, Grace," he said while gesturing forward. He was afraid; both of this strange, elderly woman standing before him, and of where they might be heading and what they might find there. Still, up till then, his life had only promised a dull, featureless future. A bit of adventure just might be interesting. And maybe he could save the world while he was at it.

*   *   *

The walking dead shambled down the roads, sidewalks, and alleyways. Homes, once brightened by the love and laughter of families and friends, were merely stepping stones for the distended corpses on their way to their final destination.

Some of the dead were elderly people. Some were husbands, wives. Some large, some small. Children were counted amongst their foul ranks, even infants, hearts lying still in their tiny, frail chests, struggled to crawl along behind their undead brethren. The towns of Toals Creek and Highland Hills were reduced to swarming masses of infected hosts, void of any memories of their past lives, uncaring for any loved ones, indifferent to who they used to be or what they had once accomplished.

A vague, but definite tint of unnatural green glistened in the daylight. Every square inch of the towns were coated in the shade, including the throngs of dead stumbling along in the streets, across front lawns, down driveways and sidewalks.

The fungus was everywhere. It dangled from trees. It crunched under the feet of the zombies. It clung to the sides of stores and houses. The metabolic by-products produced by the fungus growth were highly toxic to humans, and wholly alien in nature. They were exuded from every part of the zombie's bodies, new life forms used as carriers, as hosts to spread.

Cliff followed along behind Grace. The woman moved fairly easily through the foliage, especially for someone her age, but Cliff had a strong feeling that time probably didn't have an unbreakable contract with her like it did everybody and everything else. In fact, he suspected she was most likely much stronger and more agile than he could ever hope to be.

"So do you know exactly where were heading?"

"For the most part."

"That doesn't sound too encouraging."

"I'm sorry, but it's the truth."

Cliff fell silent. Worry and frustration chipped away at his sanity. But what choice did he have? He had to trust Grace. She was all he had, and he knew it. Without her he'd be a lost man in the middle of the forest without any clue as to where he was going.

"So you say you're the wife of Mr. Preston."

Grace stopped abruptly. Her face twisted in annoyance.

"Yes, Cliff. I believe I already said that."

Cliff backed off a bit. He didn't want to seem too pushy. The last thing he'd want would be to be left alone in the woods, especially when those things were probably roaming about.

"I'm sorry," he said quietly. "I… I didn't mean to..."

"It's all right, Cliff. I understand. Curiosity is an inbred trait to your kind."

Cliff laughed. "Yeah, I guess it is, especially when it involves surviving."

Grace smiled. "And make no mistake about it, Cliff," she said,

"This does involve your survival." A brief pause punctuated her words. "And eventually, everyone else's as well."

Cliff nodded his head as a pupil would to his teacher. He lost himself again in Grace's eyes, delicate green pools swirling within her head, enticing any who gazed upon them to partake of what they offered, of what knowledge they held.

"We must continue to travel north," Grace added, breaking the spell she held over Cliff. "Time is short. The only definite thing is that nothing is certain. Once the spores have spread, the colonization will be unstoppable." She diverted her gaze down to a thick patch of green fungus sprouting from a fallen branch. "You see, don't you? You see that the infection has already begun."

Cliff instinctively backed away from the growth. He'd seen the same substance back at the convalescent home after the zombies had already attacked. He was amazed how it was able to grow even on inanimate objects like tables and tiled floors.

The movement caught their attention simultaneously. It was approximately thirty yards away, off to their right, between a tangled thicket of brush and a large outcropping of various-sized boulders.

Cliff stood perfectly still, a cold sweat coated his body. A small part of his mind assured him that there wasn't anything really there. That it was just his imagination, and he embraced that explanation, accepting it because it was the safest route to take. "I saw something," Grace said quietly. Her green eyes narrowed. Her hands clenched into fists. Her mouth thinned into a tight grimace. "Over there, to the east, near those rocks." Her slender finger pointed.

The cold sweat on Cliff immediately increased. "You saw something too?" he asked, not really wanting to hear an answer.

"Yes. There was definitely something there."
Cliff crouched down, attempting to hide behind a rotted tree stump.

"There won't be any need for that," Grace added. "If the movement was caused by the undead, as I suspect it was, they will pay us no mind. They have to obey their calling. They cannot deter from their instructions."

Cliff quickly stood up and neurotically brushed himself off. He hated spiders ever since an aggressive burrowing wolf spider had sunk its fangs into his hand when he was a kid. Damn thing left two puncture marks right on the fleshy part of his palm. It took two weeks to completely heal. Sometimes he could swear he could still feel the itch.

The movement gradually increased in both number and animation. One became two. Two multiplied into four. Four progressed to eight. Within two short minute, there were literally dozens of shadowed figures loping through the woods.

Cliff tried not to move, too afraid to even talk, although the sheer volume of questions he had for Grace felt like a veritable tidal wave in his head.

Much to his relief, Grace was correct. The zombies, for the most part, ignored them. A few threw hungry, frustrated glances their way, but never once stopped moving along. One in particular chilled Cliff terribly.

It was a young girl, probably fifteen or sixteen years old he guessed, who trailed along behind a small group of other zombies. The hopelessness of her plight shone on her bloodless face. She had long black hair, which was tucked up into a tight ponytail, and she wore what was left of a cheerleading outfit. Cliff could still make out where *Eastside Eagles* was stitched across the front of the uniform. Darkened blood stained the letters.

But the most alarming aspect of the poor girl was the fact that she was missing both her arms; the right gone from the shoulder down and the left from just above the elbow. Red strands of gore dangled from the stumps.

Cliff watched the young girl, mesmerized by how her youthful innocence, the very heart and soul of her being, had been replaced with a rancid shell of a body, void of any humanity, depleted of memories and emotions. He found himself wondering, despite his disgust at his own thoughts, of how she had been killed and what had caused the loss of her arms. Did she still feel pain? He doubted it due to her obvious indifference toward her condition.

He stared at her as she stumbled along. His heart went out to her, to her parents, to her friends, to anyone who might have known her. He felt the weight of the situation crashing down upon him. A line from an old movie went: *When there is no more room left in Hell, the dead shall walk the Earth.* He tried to fasten the saying's meaning to the crisis, but found that he just couldn't do it. The dead were, until recently, alive. Whatever calamity had hit Michigan was the sole cause of the zombies.

His gaze switched from the dead cheerleader over to Grace. He felt a flicker of anger begin to fester in his gut. She definitely had something to do with all this, of that there was no doubt, but he couldn't do much about it because, despite her being the possible cause, she was also quite possibly the solution as well. And furthermore, if she really wasn't human there was no way to tell just what power she might possess. She could have twice his strength. Three times. Maybe she could even fly. Or have X-Ray vision... or...

Well, I guess she can at least read minds.

"It should be easier now, right?" Cliff asked. "I mean all we have to do is follow them."

Grace nodded her head. "Yes," she answered. "However, by simply following these creatures, by the time they, and we, reach their destination, the process would have already begun."

"Process? What Process? You didn't say anything about..."

"Cliff, please calm yourself."

Cliff fell silent. This adventure was quickly escalating to much more than he originally bargained for. But it was too late for him to turn back now. First of all, he wouldn't be able to find his way back. Secondly, there were zombies everywhere, some of which he even recognized: Mrs. Inkster from the Movie Mart video store, Gary Pamel, the friendly neighborhood plumber who just finished a repair to some pipes under the kitchen sink at his house, and even a old girlfriend of his, Beth something or other. He never could remember how to pronounce her last name.

Grace turned back around, facing north again. "We must bypass these creatures. We must reach the spot of origin quickly."

Cliff nodded. "All right," he conceded. "You lead, I'll follow."

Grady Preston was becoming disoriented; he was getting too old for hiking through the woods. The wind was blowing in his face. His feet were beginning to hurt. His stomach grumbled. Tree branches slapped against him, leaving painful red welts on his arms and back.

But through all his discomfort and doubt, he was urged along by the unmistakable siren song which directed every movement he made. It was a beacon calling out to him, a promise of his destiny. And all he had to do was follow it and reach the spot deemed suitable by the force for his rebirth into a god.

Grady ignored the pangs of hunger and the relentless ache of thirst and exhaustion which hounded every step he took. He'd seen several of the zombies in the area, and being comforted and encouraged by their determination in reaching their destination, began to follow them. The stench of their bodies did nothing to settle his stomach or clear his head, but he pressed on nonetheless.

And then a thought hit him. Why not feed on the fungus growths there in the woods?

He looked all around, marveling at the sickly green substance in the forest. Why he hadn't notice it before he wasn't sure, but now that he did it offered an endless supply of nourishment. And all of it right at his fingertips.

As if in reply to his revelations, the growths began to sprout mushrooms all around him, ringing his aged, frail body with their welcome presence. They were similar to the mushrooms in his room back at the home: small, pinkish, faint sport prints of lavender-colored dots on the caps, and they were dripping the same translucent goo. Without hesitating, Grady reached down and plucked one of the growths up from the ground, and with a sigh of contentment, stuffed it into his drooling mouth.

CHAPTER 19

Officer Ted Dral scrambled into the bathroom and kicked the door shut with his foot as he fell in a bloody heap on the stained toilet. The thought that it hadn't been cleaned yet shot across his mind; an irrelevant fact given his current situation. He absent-mindedly reached for his handgun but came up empty. It was a bad habit he had, one that earned him the nickname: *Drawing Dral*.

"Son of a …"

The door to the small, one- toilet bathroom rattled violently in its frame. The sheer viciousness of the assault was enough to jeopardize Officer Dral's grip on his sanity, what was responsible for the assault was enough to break it.

Rivulets of blood streamed down Ted's face. The lacerations on his forehead and scalp were easily deep enough to require stitches, but his injures didn't concern him at that moment. What did concern him however was Officers' Jammet and Szotheren who were by then hardly anything that resembled two of Highland Hills' finest, much less human beings.

"Ted? What happened buddy? Did ya fall in?" Szothern mocked through a dislodged jaw and split face. "Give someone else a chance."

Jammet growled like a rabid dog. "Yeah, Dral," he added ominously. "I gotta use the bathroom."

Ted cowered against the back wall of the bathroom, too frightened to move, his sweaty hand fondling his empty holster. He struggled to understand just what had happened. His co-workers, his fellow officers, his friends, had suddenly changed somehow, transforming right before his eyes into ravenous creatures bent on his destruction. And it all happened so fast he barely had time to escape by flinging himself into the bathroom.

He'd been leaning over his desk, pulling triplicate forms from his bottom drawer when the kid, the toddler, the dead toddler stormed through the front door of the station, spraying a greenish liquid and something that looked like a type of fungus growth across the startled faces of Jammit and Szothern. Neither man had any chance to draw his weapon or even react. They both crashed to the floor, covered in an unnatural shade of green.

The crash reverberated through the six-by-nine bathroom. A streaked mirror shattered upon impact with a chipped porcelain sink. A cheap light fixture with only one working bulb was knocked from its perch on the wall. A dingy toilet bowl scrubber leaning next to a pitted stainless-steel trash can fell on its side, followed by the trashcan.

Ted huddled in on himself, forcibly trying to gather his arms and legs tighter and tighter to his body. Sweat mingled with blood, fear with anger. If only he could make it to the radio, he could call for help. Toals Creek was close and Howell not much further than that, just to the west across the Baines River.

Jammit and Szothern were throwing anything they could get their dead hands on at the door. Fortunately for Ted it was a steel door with reinforced iron hinges and a dual-latch brass doorknob. When Sheriff Bolser took over, he had outfitted the place with heavy-duty hardware, including fourteen- gauge iron bars over all the windows and motion sensors throughout the building.

"What in the blazes is going on in here?"

It was Sheriff Bolger's voice cutting through the moans and taunts of the zombies. And for a moment, for a very brief moment, a glimmer of hope rose in Ted. But it was shattered just as quickly when he heard Bolser's voice abruptly cut off. Something rolled across the room. He assumed it was the sheriff's head.

And then he heard another sound, one that was even more unsettling than someone being decapitated. A sound which puzzled him. Why hadn't he heard it sooner?

The bullets tore through the bathroom door, spraying the small room with a shower of death. And Ted Dral, single man of 41, dedicated police officer, and budding science fiction and dark fantasy author, fell into oblivion.

*   *   *

"Just because something is impossible doesn't mean that it can't happen."

Jerry tore his swollen eyes away from Ms. Teamont's corpse. "You say something, Ryan?"

"Oh, sorry man, Ryan apologized. It's just a weird line from a book I once read. And the more I think about it, the more fitting it seems."

Jerry nodded and quickly returned his gaze back to the zombies.

"You know some of them, don't you?" Ryan asked.

"Yeah. Yeah, I do."

"I saw the way you were looking at that one woman, the one with only one hand. How do you know her?"

Jerry sighed as he fought back a complete mental break down. "She's my...she was my wife."

"Oh, I'm sorry, man. I didn't know."

"That's all right. Given the present circumstances... don't worry about it."

Ryan pulled his proverbial foot out of his mouth. It was one of his faults: always asking too many questions, never knowing when to leave well enough alone. He quickly tried to change the subject; easy enough thing to do considering that they were in the thick of a bunch of roaming zombies.

"Yeah, I'm a single guy myself. Just bought my first place too."

"Really?"

Ryan fondled his bat. "Well, I figured I'd have to be in debt to a bank somewhere eventually."

Jerry forced an insincere smile. His mind was dominated not only by the zombies and exactly where they were headed, but also by the burning worry for Martin. If only he could reach him somehow.

"I don't' suppose you have a cell phone, do you?"

Ryan laughed. "Are you kidding? First of all, you'd never get a signal out here, and secondly," his face drooped with revelation. "Secondly, anyone you'd call is probably already dead...or worse, undead."

"Yeah, I suppose you're probably right. It's just that my oldest is still out there somewhere. He has no idea what's happened to his mother or his brother and sister." Jerry's expression took on a determined look: his eyes narrowed, his mouth tightened. "If I could just talk to him, just hear his voice to know he's all right."

Pent up rage started to fester in Jerry, threatening to spill out at any moment. In the span of a few days his entire world had crumbled. And the worst part: he had no idea why. Why God Almighty would allow such a thing to occur he couldn't begin to guess.

Ryan pulled a Hershey's dark chocolate candy bar out of his bag. "I know it's not much, but…" He offered it to Jerry.

"Thanks. How'd ya know I love dark chocolate?"

"Right now any food would taste good."

Both men laughed. It was nervous, frustrated laughter, but laughter nonetheless.

Sam had been watching Jerry and Ryan from where he was crouched down behind a large, fungus-covered boulder. He found it was easier to tune out the nagging voice of his father if he listened to other people.

"You guys think we should start moving again?" he asked, his eyes darting back to the wandering corpses again. "I mean, pretty soon we'll have to, right?" His eyes pleaded with the others.

Both Ryan and Jerry nodded in agreement.

"Those things just keep coming though," Ryan noted. "I honestly don't know where the heck they're from. Was Highland Hills that populated?"

Jerry leaned forward, flinching in disgust when he noticed a thick, glistening patch of fungus pulsing near his hand. "About five or six thousand people there I think. And Toals Creek has around eight thousand, give or take."

All the color in Ryan's face drained out. "That's a lot of freakin zombies."

"I think we should get going now," Sam added, a slight trace of irritation in his tone. "For some reason those things are more interested in going somewhere than eating us."

Jerry winced. "For now."

Sam nodded. "Right. So we should follow them while we still can. The phones are probably down. Toals Creek, as well as Highland Hills, and probably Howell for that matter, are no doubt filled with corpses, and our only chance is to find out where those things are heading and why."

Ryan became annoyed, "We know all that, Einstein."

"Guys please," Jerry said, trying to keep an argument from erupting. "We are in this together and only together can we survive."

Ryan and Sam both nodded.

"Good. Now let's move out, and watch your backs."

The three men then picked up their weapons and supplies, and giving each other a nervous look, continued on their journey behind the zombies.

Approximately twenty yards away, behind a majestic oak tree stood the corpse of Wade Boulter. It watched the men move stealthily through the woods.

It followed.

CHAPTER 20

The dry streets of Toals Creek and Highland Hills were barren of life, but not movement. A few stray zombies stumbled along the roads here and there, bumping into lampposts, mailboxes, and occasionally each other. The wind flowed into their pallid faces, creating unnatural whistling noises as it shot through various empty orifices in their heads. And these universal wounds common to them were also the main cause for their calling in the woods. They simply were mechanically hindered, anatomically handicapped. It took them longer to move.

Thick patches of green fungus pocked with blossoming mushroom growths sprouted up every few feet. Some sprang from front lawns or landscaped beds while others grew upon cracked asphalt or cement driveways or parking lots. As a whole, it was a terrible sight, a painting of death and decay; nature itself tainted by an unknown and malevolent source.

A lone pair of sorrowful eyes stared out onto the streets of Toals Creek. Equal parts of grief and fear reflected in the eyes; the young girl had lost both parents and her little sister only hours before. And she had witnessed it all.

When her family came after her (dead mouths slavering for food) she'd run for her life. And finding herself cowering inside of Acorn Books (the only bookstore in town, and one she frequently visited herself), she waited out the nightmare. Her stomach was empty, her throat dry and her head ached. Dirt and bugs littered her once beautiful black hair. Her eyes were swollen with tears.

The zombie smelled the girl but could not see her; most of its face had been ripped off when it died, including both of its eyes, but it still had its nose, and it worked...for the most part.

The creature (once a loving housewife and devoted mother of four who loved to do crossword puzzles and eat frozen TV dinners) was torn between its desire to hunt down the human it smelled and following the urges, the instructions that swirled inside of what was left of its mind.

Inevitably, and much to the relief of a certain young girl hiding in a bookstore, the zombie housewife abandoned its search for prey and continued staggering along the desolate streets of Toals Creek.

*   *   *

The woods swarmed with the dead. Various forest animals (squirrels, rabbits, and an occasional deer) scurried away as soon as they detected the stench of the corpses. Bright rays of sunlight streamed through the numerous trees, occasionally illuminating the blank stare or gaping wound of a zombie.

Jerry kept as low to the ground as he could, as did Ryan and Sam. They were trailing a row of corpses, as many as eight bodies thick, and even though it was fairly obvious they weren't on the menu, they still didn't want to be seen.

"How far do you think they're going?" Ryan asked. He was not only scared but tired as well. He simply wasn't used to trudging through dense woods.

Sam looked over at Ryan. His mood, due to the absence of his father's nagging face, had lifted. "Don't know," he replied. "Hopefully it won't be too much further; my feet are starting to hurt."

Jerry was oblivious to the others' talk. His mind was focused solely on finding his remaining son. He had to find a way to talk with him. He just had to.

The blood froze in Ryan's veins when he first noticed it. Any other time and place, any other situation, he never would have believed it.

Just because something is impossible doesn't mean that it can't happen.

It was the fungus; a thin, but dense patch of growth sprinkled with small pink mushrooms. And it moved! It actually moved! And not in the sense of a tree swaying in a breeze or a boat rocking back and forth in a tempest, but it moved like something that is alive, something which is organic.

Ryan watched the growth, mouth agape, eyes fastened to the

unnatural phenomena. He'd never heard of any fungus that could move on its own, and he used to watch nature documentaries all the time growing up in Melvindale. Again he wished he had his Super Cross bike. He'd tighten his helmet straps, slip on his traverse-riding boots and roll right past all the stinking zombies. They'd never even touch him. He'd fly right past them before they knew he was even there.

"Hey, guys," he said. "You'd better have a look at this." He motioned with shaking hands at the growth.

"It's moving," Sam whispered. "It's actually moving by itself. It's freaking alive. How?" His eyes were as large as dinner plates; oily, dirt-strewn hair obscured part of his face.

"Don't touch it!" Jerry cried. "That stuff has something to do with all of this. I think it's what is bringing these things back to life. "

"But how?" Ryan asked. "And where did it come from?" He was missing his bike more and more every second. Random, happier memories of riding it flitted through his mind: ice-cold water bottle in hand, warm breeze in his face, Lou Reed humming about taking a walk on the wild side in his ears. The irony of the song title was not lost on him.

Back to the present.

"I mean that stuff wasn't around before all this happened. How could it just start growing from…"

The sheer terror reflected on Sam and Jerry's faces alone would have been enough to startle Ryan, but he also saw what they were looking at. And he nearly fell over.

The pink mushrooms began to shake, gyrating violently back and forth, lurching upward and then back down again. Lavender spots on the caps swirled into an angry red-purple shade. And then, as if in a dream, or nightmare, the stalks of the fungus extended, stretching out as if reaching for the men. All three recoiled in disgust at the display and reared back on their heels. Ryan readied his bat. Sam fondled his knife. Jerry stared, seemingly unable to react.

"Guys, I think we should get moving again," Ryan cautioned. "I think we'd be safer with the zombies."

Suddenly all around them other mushroom growths sprouted

up from patches of fungus. Translucent ooze dripped from the caps, slowly spreading across the ground, soaking dead leaves and twigs, staining nature with its stench.

Jerry stood up, followed by Ryan and Sam. He resisted the urge to draw his gun, common sense telling him that such a weapon would have little or no effect in such a situation. But he stroked it in his pocket nonetheless. If nothing else, it comforted him just to know it was there.

I've already told you boy, Sam's father chimed in from its semi-transparent perch on a twisted trunk of a nearby tree. *I've already told you. It's the new world. Only room for the dead. Only room for the dead and him.*

Sam ignored the warning.

The three men slowly got to their feet. Surveying their frightening surroundings, they stepped away from the pulsating mushrooms, being careful all the while not to step on any. Desiccated leaves and twigs crunched under their feet. In front of them, and more alarmingly behind them, zombies stumbled along, soft, guttural moans punctuating their steps.

"Come on, guys, let's go," Sam urged. His father's face still glared down at him from above, but he didn't notice it. "I say we make our way past these things quickly. Maybe then we can reach where they're going before they do." His eyes widened with excitement. He'd been looking at the situation in a different light, like it was an adventure, a journey they were all destined to make. "If we wait for these slower ones," he continued, motioning toward the lanes of corpses slowly wading through the brush, "then that fungus stuff might overtake us eventually." He kicked a particularly large mushroom which was stretching toward him with his boot, sending it flying through the damp forest air.

Jerry and Ryan looked at each other. They realized that their options were rapidly dwindling, and nodded in agreement.

The zombies were scarcely aware of the living people zigzagging through them. Only occasionally did one make a half-hearted effort to swipe at them, and even then it was almost comical in its futility.

Jerry led the way, followed by Sam. Clutching his baseball bat like it was made of gold, Sam brought up the rear. They moved quickly, efficiently, gliding through the corpses with relative ease.

Listen to me Sam; I'm your father. There is a new world…

Sam caught sight of the face. It was hanging from a drooping branch. He continued ignoring it.

Ryan couldn't help but laugh. Despite weaving around decaying corpses that would tear his throat out if given half a chance, he felt almost light on his feet. A sense of freedom settled over his tired mind. The aches and pains of his ordeal felt lifted from his shoulders, and for the first time in quite a while he felt some hope slip into his heart. It felt good.

"Come on guys," he said to Jerry and Sam as he skirted around the corpses, narrowly dodging a tall, smartly dressed man who swung the ragged remains of his left arm at him. The flailing appendage missed its target but sprayed droplets of green fungus and putrefying tissue everywhere. Ryan merely chuckled.

"These freakin things couldn't hit the side of a barn with a cannon." He wiped the residue from his arm and shoulder, discarding the handkerchief into yet another patch of fungus. "I'm getting so sick of this stuff," he complained. He kicked a patch of mushrooms. The growths disintegrated beneath his shoe. One stalk scooted away from the assault and planted itself against a stone.

"Get away from that stuff," Jerry shouted. He yanked out his gun and leveled it at the mushrooms. "We still don't know what it is yet."

"He's right," Sam chimed in. "And it's got something to do with the zombies."

Ryan took a step back; fear stretched across his face, a stark contrast to his earlier behavior.

And then the pressure gripped his ankle. And then his lower leg. And then his thigh. And it burned in its strength and intensity; it sheered clean through his pant leg.

"What the…" he cried, instinctively swinging around to see

what was assaulting him. His baseball bat dangled uselessly in his hand.

A string of mushrooms were firmly attached to his leg. They pulsed with alien life, gyrating with what could only be described as some type of agitated excitement. A few even began to swell slightly, as if bloating themselves on blood.

Ryan screamed and frantically tried to brush the clinging growths off. "They're sucking my blood!" he cried. "I can feel it! These things are sucking my blood!"

Jerry and Sam rushed to their companion. Sam wielded his knife like a pro fisherman, cleanly sliced away two of the larger caps. Cherry-colored dots remained on Ryan's leg where the things had been fastened. A thin layer of green slime coated the spots.

"Get them off of me! Get these freakin things off of me!"

"Sit still!" Sam ordered as he attempted to pry the other mushrooms off. "They're not coming off easily. I think they're fastening themselves to the skin somehow, with some type of glue or something." Loose flaps of bloodied fabric kept getting in his way.

The caps of the mushrooms were contracting and expanding, angry, swirling red on the spore prints, thin gills beneath fluttering wildly.

"Ahhh! It hurts! Get it off of me!" Ryan screamed. He still gripped his baseball bat, but didn't have the strength to use it.

Jerry felt helpless. He held the most effective weapon but couldn't utilize it. Images of Stephanie attacking him mixed with ones of their first date, their first kiss, and the birth of Wendy, Seth and Martin. He knew it wouldn't help to harbor thoughts like those but he just couldn't help himself.

Ryan's cries of pain sliced through Jerry's daydreams.

"I don't think I can get all these things off," Sam said. "They're…they're swelling, moving on him like they're alive, like they're feeding on him."

Jerry crouched down next to Ryan. He could already see the color in his face starting to drain away, slowly being replaced with a pale, soul-less façade of illness and impending death. The mere sight of it sent a fresh torrent of sadness through Jerry's heart. He'd only known Ryan a short while, being thrust together by the dire circumstances they found themselves in, but he liked him. He seemed like a good man. And they were also practically neighbors.

The growths were increasing their feeding on Ryan's leg; grotesque suckling noises accompanying the convulsing movements of the mushrooms. Blood was being siphoned out of Ryan's body and there was nothing Jerry or Sam could do about it. He was being sucked dry.

"He's dying," Sam cried out in frustration. "And I can't get these things off of him!"

"Sam," Jerry said nervously.

Sam ignored him. He was concentrating on cutting the mushrooms off of Ryan.

"Sam, I think we'd better getting going now."

"What are you talking about?"

Jerry merely pointed behind where Sam was crouched down. Sam whirled around.

A vast row of undead eyes were fastened on them.

"I think we'll have to get out of here now," Jerry repeated. "We better go!"

The ragged corpse of Wade Boulter swayed back and forth in its death-induced haze. Mosquitoes the size of pennies buzzed all around his head, attempting to locate any traces of carbon monoxide to hone in on. Blood was their goal. The females needed to eat. They needed the nourishment to lay their eggs. But Wade's blood was not circulating throughout his body, therefore it wasn't fresh, hardly what could be called healthy blood.

Wade stalked ahead, slowly, deliberately. The irresistible urges to follow the commands inside his mind were still there, and as strong as ever, but he found he was able to supersede them to a degree if he managed to incorporate other actions that were close in nature to them. He was still travelling to the location designated by the commands, but he was also seeking the ones who were still alive; his reeking gut still yearned for bloody nourishment, so much so that it wouldn't, and couldn't be denied.

The still form of his neighbor laid sprawled out on the forest floor. Flies and ants had already begun infesting the body, nibbling away bits of flesh, depositing eggs in any orifice they could. It was a grotesque but natural display.

Wade walked through the brush. He approached the corpse. One of the legs was pulsing with movement. He leaned in closer, indifferent to the sickening cracks and pops his stiffened joints produced as he did so. The body's leg was streaked with thickening blood which shimmered in the light. Pockets of weeping sores dripped from the limb, staining the flesh and producing a piercing stench. Wade did not notice it though, he merely stared at the strange display, awaiting the inevitable.

The body convulsed. First just slightly, and then more violently. Flies shot up off the corpse as it stirred from its death. The stench of the beginning processes of putrefaction drifted up and tainted the damp forest air.

Wade turned away from Ryan. A trickle of clotted fluid dripped from the empty orifice that had contained his eye. A dry, reeking hand wiped it away. He was certain Ryan would follow the commands that were by that time undoubtedly streaming into his decomposing brain. The symbiotic connection which the impending apocalypse hinged upon had already started.

In one swift, fluid movement, the fresh corpse of Ryan Connelly, twenty-four year old off-road bike enthusiast and recent first-time home buyer, leaped to its feet, steadied itself on a rock for a moment, and immediately did an about-face, leaning in the direction of the other zombies.

"I'm so hungry," he growled while surveying his surroundings as if for the first time. "Will find food." He snarled even as he started moving hypnotically north, alongside the other dead. Evil frustration played out across the dead man's face. A faint residue of his previous life was also present, one which consisted of his love of mountain bikes, baseball, and barbeques.

But those fond memories, those past loves were soon to be

erased. The growths were swelling into alien-tainted fruiting bodies within their host, releasing their pathogens. They were producing bioactive compounds, similar to the mycotoxins Earth-bound fungi produce. But these were far more dangerous. These pathogens were not bound by nature's design.

Wade stood in a small clearing, flanked by glistening mushroom growths. He trained his remaining eye on the vast hoards of zombies wading through the woods. He did not know their, or his destination, or why they were being drawn toward it.

In the distance a strange clicking noise suddenly cut through the forest. It was rhythmic, almost like a steady beat, only slightly more sporadic. The birds that were clacking out their mating calls were totally ignorant of the undead carnage playing out below them. They merely continued with their rituals.

The noises caught Wade's attention. He tilted his head in the direction of the sounds, momentarily pondering their origins.

And then it happened: his hands began to tap against his legs in synchronization with the bird's mating calls. And inside his body, his dead body, a primal fire was kindled. And within the span of a few seconds, it roared into a raging pyre of recollection.

Wade started tapping his hands to the beat, occasionally adding an accent here, a ghost note there. And in a minute or two he was creating a melodic symphony of rhythm, all fueled by refreshing memories of his past drumming days.

His decay-ravaged face split into a toothy grin. His hands were banging more furiously by then, each makeshift note beautiful ringing in his ears. Every space between each note was an anxious waiting period desiring to be filled.

The tempo increased. Quarter notes slid into eights, and then inevitably, sixteenths. Wade played on top of the beat. He played beneath it. He eyed illusions of shiny brass cymbals, his cymbals, perched on their heavy-duty chrome stands, positioned accordingly around his imaginary drum set. He crashed his hands into them, simulating crescendos at the end of each measure.

But the joy Wade experienced from his rhythmic trip down

memory lane was not the only significant aspect of his new behavior.

He remembered.

He remembered a part of his previous life and was able to embrace it, to grasp all that the memories had of offer. And this represented freedom of thought on his part; although he still felt the restrictive and domineering effects of the spores multiplying rapidly in his body and the swelling in every cell of his corpse, controlling his movements, directing him to the unknown destination he was programmed for. But for the first time since he had died, he thought for himself. He and he alone chose to turn the common mating calls from some birds into a fairly imaginative rhythm, one that he recalled pounding out on his drum set.

Wade cocked his head back as if to let out a laugh. He wanted to release the joy, the satisfaction he felt from his newfound independence, his hew strength, but only a raspy groan escaped through his dry, cracked lips. His vocal cords simply did not function properly anymore.

Frustration welled up inside of him, threatening to topple all he had recently achieved. But Wade staved off the emotion. If he were to allow his anger to get the better of him, he would be doomed to travel the inevitable path the other zombies were following. Even in his current state he could see that.

Looking around, Wade noted how the rows of the undead were gradually increasing their movements. A young girl who couldn't have been more than twelve or thirteen years old pushed past him. Both of her arms were missing, strings of clotted gore trailing from the pink stumps, and what used to be her upper back was now only a hollowed out cavity. It almost appeared that something had taken a huge bite out of her. A ragged doll, red button eyes dangling loosely by single threads, was still clutched in the girl's ashen hand.

Did she still harbor a trace of her past life?

Perhaps. Perhaps not.

Wade pondered the irony of it all. It didn't really matter if the girl still had memories of her former life or not. She was a slave to a higher purpose. A mere soldier in a vast army of dead, following orders like any good military drone would do.

The thick fungus was blanketing Wade's feet. It squirmed with life, alien life, inching its way up toward his rotting legs. Tubular, thread-like tendrils stretched up from the mass and wavered in the tainted air. They sensed independent thought, rebellion, escape from their control. The tips of the tendrils pulsed with cellular activity. Aggregated vesicles throbbed with mindless abandon. Further infection was imminent.

Wade bent down and brushed the fungus away. A few of the tendrils stuck fast, furiously attempting to pump their pathogen into the host, but they were ripped away. Tiny blades of serrated tooth-like structures pulled bits of decayed flesh away with them.

The woods were by then congested with wandering zombies. Thousands of mobile corpses constantly bumped into each other, some toppling over, only to be trod upon by others without regard.

Wade thought for a moment. He knew what he must do. With a violent jerk of his hand, he crammed it straight down his throat. Digits jostled around for a moment or two before finally finding purchase. Without hesitation he ripped his hand back out of his mouth. Blackened teeth showered the ground. The split remains of a swollen tongue were cast aside. Gore-streaked lips were shredded to fleshy mulch.

Wade held his hand up to his face. His remaining eyeball focused on what it held. Satisfaction coursed through the rotting empty canals of his body.

It was a mushroom. A small, pink mushroom with white gills and a light purple cap. Streaks of gray and black slime dripped off of it, residual tissue matter from Wade. It shimmied back and forth like a small animal trying to escape from a trap.

Wade grinned. His brain had decayed to the point where he was having trouble controlling his motor functions, but he still swelled with pride. He managed to achieve independence. The thing he held in his hand was special, one of a kind. It was unique. It was the first of its kind. It possessed traits that the others did not. It was the seed from above.

The mushroom squirted foul-smelling goo between Wade's

fingers when he squeezed it. The bulbous cap oozed outward before collapsing under the pressure. Light green mist drifted upward from the ruined growth and quickly dispersed into the forest air.

When Wade finally released his grip, the soupy remains of the mushroom dripped off of his hand, settling on the forest floor in a blotchy pool of filth. A quick rubbing from his shoe smeared any leftover traces into oblivion.

CHAPTER 22

"For a woman your age, you sure move quickly."

Cliff regretted the words as soon as they left his mouth. The last thing he wanted to do was offend Grace, both because he wasn't brought up to be rude to people and also he'd be up a creek without a paddle if she left him to fend for himself. Even if the zombies didn't get him, the forest surely would.

"I'll take that as a compliment," Grace coolly replied while navigating over a hollowed out tree trunk. "As I said before, we must move quickly. The walking dead will not harm us. They are already spoken for, commanded to do a bidding higher than anything on this... this planet."

Cliff nodded as he stretched out for leverage from a large, twisted branch. He was working his way around a particularly thick patch of mushrooms, at least eight or nine inches deep. Several of the stalks reached up as his foot passed over them.

"So you're really from another planet?" He didn't like to be nosy, but given the current circumstances he felt the question was legitimate.

Grace didn't stop moving, but responded without delay.

"If that is how you wish to perceive my presence here."

Cliff nodded in satisfaction as he made his way through the brush. "What's your planet like?"

A rather large zombie lumbering past them momentarily diverted his attention. The man had been very well built, but now his skin sagged on his body; pale strips swinging loosely in the breeze.

"It's a beautiful place, void of such things as these horrible creatures." Her face stretched into a frown. "I miss being there, where one can grow without hindrance."

"What do you mean 'grow'?"

"Cliff, I'm different from you. My species have organic traits that allow us to spread our presence across the cosmos." She looked back at her young companion. "Suffice to say that we are different."

Cliff dropped the subject. He burned with curiosity, as anyone would have, but thought better of asking too many questions. Grace might become annoyed, or worse still, he might find out information that he didn't want to know in the first place. He decided it would be best to simply shut his mouth and follow her. She obviously knew what to do.

*   *   *

Grady instantly felt better. The mushrooms provided nourishment to his aged relic of a body just as they had back at the home. He felt energy coursing through his body. He felt renewed, revitalized, recycled. "Now I can continue toward my destiny," he mused.

A pair of twin zombies (two middle-aged women, one missing most of her abdomen, the other the left side of her body from her ear down to her hip) stumbled by, putrid gore clotting with decay, filling the cavities. The two still closely resembled one another despite their gaping wounds and advanced state of decomposition.

Grady recoiled in disgust; the stench put him off, curling his nose hairs and churning his stomach, but he also felt a connection with every aspect the dead women possessed. They would be a part of him, an undeniable link to his future.

Off in the distance several more zombies wandered along. They moved in clusters, occasionally grunting in hunger, and always sporting blank expressions tinged with frustration. Even in their unfeeling, dead state, they apparently still resented being forced into servitude.

Impatience suddenly slipped into Grady's mind. It was tempered by uncertainty, but he embraced it nevertheless. A newfound urgency took over his mindset. He must get to his destination quickly. He must start the process. Any more delay could prove disastrous.

The movement caught his eye: two figures, about a hundred yards away off to the east, wandering along a line of twisted oak trees. They were obviously trying to avoid being detected, although the zombies didn't do anything to attack them regardless.

Grady crouched down where he stood, his gut churning with the remains of the mushrooms he'd eaten. The partially digested growths stretched upward within him. He could feel them bending and twisting, gyrating back and forth in an effort to infest the untainted ones nearby. He patted his midsection lightly.

"Settle down, my little friends," he consoled. "We'll get them. We'll get them soon enough."

He leaned over and snatched up an oblong-shaped stone. It was generously covered with fungus, but it still possessed the main aspect that could make it a dangerous weapon: weight. It was heavy enough to easily cave in the skull of a man. Or two men.

CHAPTER 23

"Do you think he'll come back as one of those things?" Jerry asked.

Sam looked back at his companion. His eyes were red and swollen, both from the stench of the zombies and the tears he constantly fought back. Ryan was a good man, and he found himself missing him already.

"Yeah, I'd say so," he replied sadly. "But I wasn't gonna stick around to find out."

The words stung Jerry, but he was forced to agree with them.

"I wish we at least had time to bury him."

"Me too, but he'd probably just dig his way back out."

Again Jerry resigned his feelings in agreement. Since the nightmare began, he found himself doing that more and more. A brand new world had been thrust upon him, and its inhabitants were rotting corpses who had already taken his wife and two of his children. Now they were threatening to take something else as well. Something almost as important to him as his family: his sanity. He struggled to keep up with Sam.

"Do ya know the first thing that me and my oldest are gonna do when we get away from all of this mess?"

Sam momentarily stopped in his tracks. He swung a puzzled look back at Jerry. Despite their situation, he was still curious about what his companion was going to say. "You mean your kid in college?"

"Yeah, Martin. The first thing we're gonna do is catch a Tigers game, and then go into Greektown for dinner. And then if the weather's nice enough, we'll have a beer or two along the Riverwalk by the Renaissance Center."

A pleasant look of remembrance flashed across Jerry's face, brightening his color and making his eyes sparkle.

"You ever been there, Sam?"

Sam shook his head as he took a swig from a dirty water bottle. He wasn't looking at Jerry; his eyes were locked on a small cluster of zombies in front of him and off to his left. They were beginning to leak a disgusting substance, most likely a mixture of blood, rotted tissue, and fungus residue.

"No," he finally mumbled with only minor interest. His mind, as well as his eyes, focused on the zombies.

Jerry wiped his forehead. It felt like he removed a hundred pounds of dirt and grime from his face with the simple gesture. It felt so good he nearly fainted. A fond, distant memory of taking hot showers rolled across his mind.

"It's a great place. Downtown is really cleaned up nice. You should go down there sometime. Ford Field, Comerica Park, Greektown Casino, Fox Theater, Hockytown Café..."

Sam nodded. "Yeah, I've heard there's a lot to do there. Just haven't had a chance to check it out yet."

Jerry frowned. The realization that all those great places he'd visited so many times in the past, all those memories, most likely meant nothing now. The dead probably inhabited them, scavenging for living people to prey on, stumbling through and around the beloved establishments spreading the stench of death. He envisioned the nightmarish scene in his head: the cobblestone streets between Hockeytown Café and Comerica Park sprayed with foul green fungus. The Detroit Athletic Club, its decades of prominence amongst the social elite long since vanished, towering over swarming masses of reeking undead. Hart Plaza, once a veritable mecca of gathering, both musical and culinary, now only housing the guttural collapse of civilization in all its rotting glory.

And the worst part was that the zombies had no appreciation for the beauty of mankind's achievements, either architecturally or spiritually. They simply meandered back and forth, up and down, in and out of their surroundings, completely unaware or caring just where they were.

Jerry felt his resolve to carry on slipping away. Only the forced thoughts of finding his remaining child and hopefully stopping the plague kept his feet moving, although slowly and without much strength. Determination seemed like a commodity that was harder to grasp with each step he took.

"You okay, Jerry?" Sam felt bad for the guy. Losing your kids and wife and then being attacked by them after they died had to be tough. And then all the memories he had of Detroit.

Jerry nodded. "Yeah, I'm fine. It's just that I'm getting so sick of all this crap."

"Tell me about it." Sam thought how he not only had to deal with the walking dead trying to eat him alive, but also the leering face of his father nagging him at every turn.

Jerry sighed. He watched the twisted wreckage of an elderly woman zombie waddle by. She wore a yellow blouse which he surmised had been white at one time, and her slacks were torn and tattered, revealing strips of shredded, pale flesh. A gaping hole was all that remained of her neck. Jerry winced in disgust first at the smell, and then when he noticed the tiny pink mushrooms blooming in her body. The growths swelled and contracted.

He slipped a bottle of water out of his bag. "I am getting so sick of this," he repeated. "Just so sick of it."

CHAPTER 24

Cliff watched in amazement as a small deer scampered by. It was somewhat plump for such a young doe, with pure white spots decorating its hind section. Its glossy black eyes were fixed on all of the movement around it, but could do little about it. There simply were too many of the zombies milling about. The doe had apparently realized its best chance of survival was to try to remain as still as possible. Escape was a dangerous and potentially fatal option.

But what truly amazed Cliff were the zombies that did notice the deer and ignored it. Sure, the walking dead hadn't paid them any attention either in quite a while as well, but this deer had been unfortunate enough to find itself at one time wedged between two zombies. They could have easily reached out and gripped the animal by the neck with minimal effort. It would have been a free lunch.

Grace had stopped momentarily, studying Cliff as he watched the deer.

"It is safe, as we are."

"But why don't they attack it? Or us?" Cliff asked, his gaze still locked on the doe.

"Because they cannot attack that animal no more than you could stop breathing, or blinking your eyes, or eating."

Cliff felt relieved in a way; he'd grown accustomed to the smell of rot and the sight of decay walking along beside him. "I guess so," was all he was able to say.

Grace's smile instantly switched to an expression of anxiety. Her eyes narrowed with determination, tightening her face with the look of a solider about to step onto a battlefield.

Cliff looked up. He'd heard the sound as well, as was clearly reflected on his face.

"You heard that too?" he asked. "It wasn't just me?"

Grace didn't respond. Her eyes darted from side to side, up, down, scanning the immediate area for the source of the sound. Suddenly she resembled a hungry lion stalking zebra, wholly intent on accomplishing her mission. Without another word, she began to edge her way forward, silently navigating through the brush.

Cliff decided the best and only thing to do would be to follow her. He took one step, then two. And by his third the sound yet again rained down in the forest from the distance.

Grace stopped her progress and turned back to Cliff. "They have arrived. We must hurry. Perhaps it is already too late."

A terrible sinking feeling descended on Cliff. He hadn't felt one like it since he'd first encountered his neighbor in his living room. It settled over his heart like a wet blanket over a candle, effectively snuffing out any hope still there.

"What do you mean?" he asked quietly. He was afraid of what answer he might hear.

"They have arrived at the spot. Some of their numbers have successfully reached the area. Those sounds are calls from the Home Growth to its servants. It's sending out a beacon to help others reach it quickly, particularly my husband. He is the key. He is what is required to propagate the species."

Cliff looked down at his feet. He didn't know what to say or how to react. The news sliced him wide open, spilling out his strength and clouding his mind. For the first time, he actually missed his former life. It was boring, but at least it was safe.

"I... I....what should we do?"

Grace smiled. "There is need to worry, of that I won't lie to you, Cliff, but I believe..." She paused for a moment as a zombie, which was missing both its legs, crawled by on its split-open belly. A trail of glistening viscera was left in its wake. After the corpse dragged itself past them, she continued.

"I believe we still have time. If only a few have successfully located the area, and if we can get there quickly enough, the process could possibly be reversed."

Cliff stared hard at her. His head was pounding, threatening to crack wide open at any moment and his neck and lower back were stiff. He felt like an eighty year-old man, and it showed on his face.

"Come now, Cliff," Grace commanded. "We must increase our pace. We no longer need to follow these creatures. The sounds from the

Home Growth itself will guide us." And with those words, she spun around and darted off, sidestepping several particularly decomposed zombies, one of which, a gaunt, mostly intact teenage girl, took a weak swipe at her.

Cliff took a deep breath and followed close behind Grace. Staying near her offered a small measure of security, although hardly enough to set his mind at ease. But he had no choice.

*   *   *

Wade plodded around the other zombies with the ease of an athlete moving about statues. The other dead occasionally groaned or growled at him, but for the most part, were easily pushed aside. Wade had heard the sounds emanating from deeper in the woods. The echoes still rung through his rotted cranium, spilling their messages into what intelligence and reasoning he still possessed. He sorted through their meaning as best he could.

The memories still hung around his neck like a sack of bricks: the smiling faces of his children, his beautiful wife, his faithful dog. All of the images were still clear in his head. They were all happy, everyone grinning, laughing, sharing time together; but the reality of what he had done, of what he had been compelled to do, crept into his mind as well, staining the beloved memories with blood and pain.

Wade focused on what he must do, on where he must go. It wasn't easy, but
it was still a preferable alternative to the painful thoughts of his past deeds. Each step he took was like being a toddler again. He had to struggle to maintain his balance. He was moving in the right direction, of that there was no doubt, but it still was like trying to locate a ghost. The sounds were clear and easily distinguishable but vague nonetheless. They drifted up into the vast emptiness of the forest.

And then something occurred to him. The other zombies were increasing their movements. They bumped and jostled around each other as if they were in some distorted type of race.

But what was at the finish line? What possible prize could be waiting for the one who got there first?

Wade stood still for a moment or two, surveying the woods all around him. The pull that had directed him so far was gone, replaced with his own free will, and so he did not follow the other undead. He merely watched them stumble by; he was waiting for the most opportune time to move.

The large, elderly zombie fell face first into a thick patch of pulsating mushrooms. The growths muffled its impact, sending small, greenish clouds of spore vapor into the forest air.

Wade swung his dead gaze over to where the creature was. He staggered toward it as quickly as he could.

The entire side of the man's head had been sheared away by a heavy, mottled stone. Bits of slimy brain matter and bloody tissue were scattered across the ground as if shot from a spray can, and a mangled ear, complete with a small gold crucifix dangling from it, lay atop a moss-laden tree stump. Wade watched as a thin, gray squirrel snatched the disgusting morsel and scampered away with it out of sight.

The origin of the stone perplexed Wade, and he immediately scanned the neighboring areas for the fallen zombie's assailant. Within a few seconds, he saw him. There, cowering behind a huge tree trunk was an aged, crooked old man.

He was easily in his eighties, and he sported an evil grimace wholly uncharacteristic of such an elderly person. The fire of hatred and determination burned in his glassy eyes like a man a third of his age. Green spittle dribbled down his wrinkled chin, staining the front of his tattered clothes. His right arm hung limply by his side, telltale evidence that he had thrown the rock.

Wade turned and began to advance on the old man. His mouth was agape; the chipped remnants of his teeth clattered together like a car engine in need of a tune-up. Faint tapping noises drifted up every time his teeth came together.

The old man quickly noticed him and scrambled to retrieve another stone. Angry curses shot out of him in bunches, one segueing into another. He'd been aiming for the two living people, not just another zombie. He had no doubt that there would be enough of them left of fulfill his fate so the one that had fallen didn't distress him too much. But it did bring his location to the attention of the other zombie, the one that was now coming toward him.

Grady knew that this particular zombie was not like the other ones. The remaining eye it possessed shone with a glint of intelligence, of free will, of freedom of thought. It sensed the threat nearby, and reacted to it.

The stone fell from Grady's hand, landing on the soil with a soft thud. He backed up slowly at first before scampering away as fast as his frail legs would carry him. Wade simply stood and watched him run.

And then he noticed two other people. They were about fifty yards ahead of the fleeing old man. They weren't among the dead zombies, which was clearly evident from their movements, and they were stealthily making their way in the same direction as the zombies were, and the old man, and himself.

CHAPTER 25

How many times do I have to tell ya Son, the half-transparent face snorted from a dangling branch. Rows of tiny pink mushrooms dotted the tree limb, decorating the image of Sam's father like acne on a teenager's face. They pulsated with each word that was spoken. *It's the new world that is coming. There's only room in it for the dead.*

Sam paused in his stride for a brief moment and looked up into his father's face. "Don't you also mean him?" he shot back. "Don't you mean only room for the dead and him?"

Yes, yes, his father replied with a sly grin. A particularly bulbous mushroom had planted itself dead center on his forehead, a thin trickle of green fluid was leaking from its cap. *That's right, Son. That's right. And him too. The dead and him too.*

"You talking to someone?" Jerry asked quietly while nervously glancing around. Over time he'd grown somewhat accustomed to moving amongst the living dead, but as they neared the area where the zombies were apparently heading to, he didn't want to draw any more attention to themselves than was absolutely necessary.

Sam glanced over at Jerry. "It's nothing. Sometimes I imagine that my dad is talking to me. Haven't seen him in quite a while now, so I guess it's just my mind playing tricks on me." He could only hope that Jerry wouldn't think he was crazy. Jerry laughed. "Don't worry, Sam. After all we've been through, after all we're probably gonna have to go through, I don't think talking to your dad is on our agenda for things to worry about."

Sam looked up at his dad. "You hear that?" he snapped. "I don't have to keep you hidden anymore." Satisfaction swelled within him. "I don't have to pretend I'm not seeing you anymore."

The face of Sam's father began to dissipate, gradually fading away into nothingness. *Suit yourself, Son,* it warned. *But remember, only room for the dead. Only room for…*

"Wait!" Sam suddenly cried out. "Before you leave. Who is the other one you said would be in the new world along with the dead? Who were you talking about?"

So now you'll listen to me, his father said callously. *Look behind you and you'll see your answer.*

Sam whirled around, his swollen eyes focusing on the streams of zombies and their frustrated, hungry expressions. And then he noticed the man running in his direction, a small hunched over man who was cursing as he went. Jerry looked back as well.

"Who in God's name is that?"

Sam shook his head. "Don't know, but whoever he is he's coming right at us."

Both men readied themselves to confront the old man.

"Outta my way," Grady warned as he skirted past Sam and Jerry. "I've got to get to the spot!"

From a distance more strange noises erupted. They sounded like a huge plunger being lifted out of a commode. The intense sucking noise reverberated throughout the woods, effectively drowning out all wildlife in the area. Trees shook from the clamorous sounds. The echoes were deafening.

"I hate to say it, but I think we need to get to where that's coming from," Jerry said in resignation. His mind was focused solely on seeing Martin again, and he knew deep down that confronting whatever was at the heart of this mess might be the only way he'd be able to. If they didn't stop this disaster at its source, it would surely spread, and then he'd never make it back to Martin. There probably wouldn't be anything left there…or anywhere else given enough time.

Sam shook his head briefly as if expelling the residual traces of his father's image from his mind. "Yeah, I know," he said. "I don't think it's too far ahead; maybe a couple of hundred yards or so."

Jerry nodded. "Come on," he urged, jumping up and pulling Sam along by the arm. "Let's go."

*   *   *

The old man was easily twenty to thirty yards ahead of them, but he wasn't their objective. True, he'd tried to kill them, and the way he was moving was disturbing to say the least (a twisted gait reminiscent of a drunken sailor scrambling along a midnight sidewalk), but there were far worse things in the woods besides a crazy old man throwing rocks. There were still zombies all around them. People who had, until just a short time earlier, been husbands and wives, sons and daughters, mothers, fathers, brothers, sisters, friends, co-workers. And now they were mindless machines following some bizarre and mysterious agenda.

Sam followed close behind Jerry, clutching his hunting knife in a sweaty hand. A jagged stone was in his other hand.

"Do you still see that crazy old man?"

Jerry didn't respond. He had his eyes locked on a section of woods up ahead of them. His mind alternated between finding Martin, Stephanie, Wendy and Seth, his house (now a ruined, deserted monument), and the faint green glow emanating from a depressed crevice between a copse of gnarled trees. Thick brush encircled the trees, enclosing the strange cavity that appeared not to have been sculpted by Mother Nature at all.

"I think we're just about there," Jerry mumbled under his breath. He pointed.

Sam peered past his companion into the glow. His stomach twisted in knots and his head began to spin with the implications of what lay before them.

"Well," he sighed, "I guess we better get a move on. Judging by the looks of the zombies, we don't have a heck of a lot of time."

Jerry nodded, never taking his eyes off of the green glow. He cradled his pistol in a shaking hand and started moving forward through the brush.

"Do you really think we have a chance to stop this thing?" Sam asked quietly. His father's face had not appeared in a while and he found himself missing it in a way. At least it was a familiar face, although irritating. Talking to it helped to steady his nerves…a little.

"Frankly, I don't know," Jerry replied. "But I'll tell you one thing though. We'll put a dent in it if nothing else. I've lost my wife and two of my kids to this mess and I intend on getting back to my remaining son."

"Well, I don't have any son to live for," Sam replied. "But I wanna live just the same."

"Amen."

"You got that right."

Jerry froze in his tracks when a small zombie girl, who had been in the middle of a larger group, abruptly stopped in front of him. It turned to face him.

"W…Wendy?"

Jerry's youngest cocked her decayed head to one side. Her eyes were empty black pools reflecting no warmth, no emotion, and no recognition of her own father. How he had failed to notice her before he couldn't understand; she had been only twenty or thirty feet in front of him all along.

The pistol jumped in his hand and the top portion of Wendy's head exploded, spilling greasy brain matter across the green, mushroom-laden ground.

"May God forgive me," Jerry sobbed into his forearm. "May God forgive me."

Sam stood still behind Jerry, stunned that his companion had enough courage, enough strength to end his own daughter's zombie existence without hesitation.

"I… I just couldn't see her like that anymore. I just couldn't. She wasn't my little girl anymore. I had to put her out of her misery." Jerry looked up at Sam, his face red with tears. "You understand, don't you, Sam? You understand why I did what I did, don't you?"

Sam nodded and patted Jerry on the back. "Of course I do, Jerry. It took a lot of courage to do that."

Jerry looked at the darkening horizon. The orange ribbon cast by the setting sun contrasted strongly with the unnatural green glow from the crevice. As a whole, it created a surrealistic mixture of colors.

"You know," he said quietly. "This whole mess might prove to be just the spark my novel needs."

Sam glared at him with wide, disbelieving eyes.

"If you say so, Jerry," he mumbled.

"Yeah. Killer fungus from outer space. Unlikely heroes cast

together under stressful situations. Heartbroken father searching for his son after losing the rest of his…the rest of his family."

Sam quickly realized that Jerry was on the brink of a meltdown. He seized his companion by the shoulders and shook him vigorously.

"That's right, Jerry. Heroes. We're heroes. And you have to get back to your

son alive. Do you hear me? Alive. Martin will need his dad. And you'll need him."

Jerry straightened up, cuddling his gun to his chest.

"You're right. No time for grieving now."

"So you're all right?"

"I'm fine. Now let's go and see just what all the commotion is by that green light."

The two men moved forward then, unaware of the headless corpse of Wendy struggling to its feet behind them.

CHAPTER 26

Grace was moving along even more quickly than she had before. Cliff was on her heels, but was having trouble keeping up. Sweat trickled down his dirty face in thin streams. He wiped his brow repeatedly with his arm.

The fear that had settled in his gut was becoming all consuming, sapping what little strength and determination he still possessed. The relative safety he'd felt from being near Grace was thinning.

"Can you see anything yet?"

Grace shook her head. "Not yet, Cliff, but I sense, due to the density of the undead creatures about us and their increased movements, that we are nearing the location."

Cliff didn't answer. He was watching a large gathering of zombies off to his left. The monsters were getting closer to him and Grace. Several of them even shot frightening glances in their direction.

"There," Grace suddenly said, "that will lead us directly to the Home Growth." She pointed at a narrow track between two small risings, up on either side. The path was clear of any mushrooms, but the dangerous growths coated both sides.

They navigated through dense brush with meandering undead forms stumbling along beside them. Cliff wondered not only what awaited them at this Home Growth spot but what they could do to stop it. They had no weapons and no army. But they did have Grace, who obviously had inside information about the situation. Knowledge was usually more valuable than sheer brute strength.

As they wound their way down the narrow path, a sharp smell drifted into the air. It mingled with the damp rot of the zombies, but was even more pungent, and it stung their eyes.

"This just keeps getting better and better," Cliff said sarcastically.

Grace kept her eyes focused on the winding path in front of them. Her face was tightened with determination and her breath was steady and light. She was nearing her destination and possibly her fate.

"The smell is getting stronger," Cliff complained. "It stinks like something burning, like bodies maybe." A random, but sickening comparative thought slipped into his mind before he could stop it: his barbeque back home. The image of it in his head, combined with the stench, made him feel like vomiting.

"We must be strong," Grace reminded in a stern tone. "I can see plumes of smoke rising from thickets of trees up ahead. We are very close now Cliff. Very close."

Cliff nodded and followed close behind her, his stomach cramped with hunger despite the terrible smell. They followed the path while it skirted huge rocks and dangling tree limbs before they descended gradually into a deep depression. The ground was becoming oily in consistency, changing into a greasy sheet of green fungus. Their feet squelched in the substance.

Eventually the path began to wind higher and higher until it dissolved into a near-vertical outcropping of stone. Dozens of zombies stumbled close behind them, following their lead to the Home Growth.

Cliff was becoming more and more nervous. "Grace, we'd better hurry up," he mentioned just as a middle-aged woman zombie dressed in tattered blue jeans and a frayed yellow blouse took a lazy swipe at him as she stumbled along. The entire left side of her abdomen was missing, strings of rotted tissue hanging in the bloody space like Christmas tree lights.

Grace ignored him. Her eyes were fixed on the top of the ridge directly in front of them.

"Cliff, you must hoist me above this rising. I am unable to reach the top by myself."

Cliff nodded and came up behind her. He cupped his hands together to form a crude step. Grace stepped back and positioned her right foot into Cliff's hands, steadying herself on his shoulders. And with one smooth motion Cliff lifted her up.

She was surprisingly heavier than he expected. It felt like she was made of heavy machinery, firm and unyielding. He grunted with the exertion.

"You...you see anything yet?"

Grace scanned the landscape from her new vantage point. The green glow reflected off her face.

"Yes, it is there. We have reached the..." The words fell from her mouth as her body collapsed to the ground. Looking up, she cleared the dirt from her face; dark shapes were gathering in growing numbers, blotting out the trees, choking off any trace of clean air left with their stench.

Grace shot to her feet. Cliff was sprawled on the ground off to her left. She grasped him by the arm, and pulled him to his feet. Behind them, over the ledge, silver flashes of lightening forked through the sky. Distant thunder rumbled from overhead, heralding a violent storm. The gore-streaked faces of the dead shone briefly in the young tempest.

"Cliff! You must wake up!" Grace cried through the swirling winds. She smacked him once across the cheek, and as if awakening from a long night's sleep, Cliff slowly opened his bloodshot eyes.

"Grace? W...where are we?"

"Quickly! Raise me up over the ledge."

Cliff shook his head to clear his mind and cupped his hands together again. Grace placed her foot in them and was lifted steadily upward until she was out of the dark maw that had been the path. Below, growling zombies surrounded Cliff.

"Why are they getting aggressive again?" he asked nervously. A young boy, seven, possibly eight years old at most, swung his one remaining arm at him, narrowly missing the side of his face. The dead boy moaned in frustration. "Before, they only seemed interested in getting to that Home Growth spot. Now it looks like they want to eat us again."

Grace was mesmerized by what she was seeing over the top of the ledge. Her eyes were glazed over by the beautiful display.

"Grace? I really could use a hand here. Grace?"

Cliff's pleas for help snapped her out of her trance. She reached down, and gripping Cliff's hand tightly, pulling him up to safety. Scores of undead hands wavered from below in futile efforts to reach their lost prey.

Cliff stood up and brushed himself off. The close call with

death had left him rattled. Taking a few deep breaths, he pushed aside the fear and disbelief in his mind.

"Boy, that was a close one. So now what do we…"

The dense glow from the Home Growth throbbed with alien malevolence. It threatened to tear the fabric of time and space apart simply from its impossibility. The very fact that it actually existed exuded sheer power. It pulsed from a cavernous depression not more than thirty feet from where Cliff and Grace stood. A heavy ring of brush encircled the spot, a sickening vortex from which no warmth escaped. A dark shape the size of a small man squirmed near its outer rim. It flailed its arms high above its head as if performing some ritualistic dance.

Grace looked over at Cliff. Her eyes shone with a sadness that he had never encountered before. It was deep and penetrating, radiating up from the depths of her soul.

"Is…is that it?"

Grace nodded sorrowfully. "Yes, it is. It is my husband."

Cliff cleared his throat, exchanging glances between the unnatural display and the burgeoning masses of zombies gathering below them. "What in God's name is he doing?"

Looking back at her husband, Grace coolly replied, "He is realizing his true potential."

"Potential? He's the key to this whole mess right? We have to stop him."

Dozens of zombies had gathered around Grady. Cliff's stomach recoiled in horror when he recognized two of them. One wore a bloodstained white lab coat and still had a chrome stethoscope hanging around its neck. Green fungus clung to the stained metal like splotches of paint. The other zombie was a middle-aged woman who wore a striped blouse with a tattered windbreaker over it. Long, parallel strips of fabric were missing from the back of the coat, apparently caused by something with claws. A dog perhaps? Bits of green-tinged flesh poked out from the tears. Cliff guessed a combination of the fungus and the natural decomposition of the body attributed to the ghastly shade.

The female corpse swung its baleful gaze up directly at Cliff and Grace. Most of its face had been chewed off, but Cliff still recognized the woman. He remembered talking with her just a short while earlier at the convalescent home.

With what was left of her face, Jane jerked a distorted grin in the direction of Cliff. The malevolence in the expression was obvious, as was the hunger and the frustration. She, like all the other undead, was fastened to the mysterious force directing her actions. She was powerless to resist it.

Cliff wanted to back away, an instinctive reaction for anyone, but the ground behind him dropped off sharply; a mass of crawling zombies still struggled to reach him and Grace.

"Come now, Cliff, we must move forward," Grace said as she grasped him by the arm tightly. So much so that Cliff felt a new wave of concern overtake his already frightened mind. He pulled Grace's hand off, shrinking in disgust when he noticed it was comprised of thick, green mushroom-like growths. The bulbous caps pulsed with alien life.

"What the…"

Cliff felt his heart leap into his throat. The cavernous expressions which manifested all around him bore down like a heavy thunderstorm, each penetrated Cliff's soul with clearly evident malice. But not a single one of them matched the evil visage that radiated from the person standing right next to him: Grace herself.

I said we must move forward," Grace repeated in a darker tone. "My husband awaits us. It's been so long, too long since we've seen each other. Her deep green eyes expanded to such a degree that they threatened to split her face wide open.

Cliff felt himself grow faint. The mundane life he'd been forced to leave behind beckoned to him. He yearned for it more than ever, wishing only to bask in its boring glory. How he yearned for a simple average day, void of zombies or killer mushrooms.

"You see, Cliff," Grace continued while wrapping her now elongated arms around him. "My husband believes I passed away in a fire decades ago. He thinks he is all alone, and that he must fulfill his destiny by himself." Her thin lips curled into the mockery of a smile.

"But he is mistaken. I have always been here. My kind needs to….hibernate, so to speak, in order to allow our spores to germinate properly. It takes many years, but eventually the time comes for change." She pulled Cliff close to her and opened the dark cavity that was her mouth impossibly wide. Cliff flinched in disgust at the rows of writhing mushrooms inside the maw. "And that time is now."

CHAPTER 27

The corpse of Wade Boulter navigated its way around the pillars of rock. Thick stubs of long-dead tree trunks jutted up from the fungus-covered forest floor, pulsating mushroom heads dotting every square of their surfaces. A host of black, distorted figures scrambled along as well, their dead expressions showing no hint to their past lives or thoughts. One such corpse was still dressed in an officer's uniform. *Highland Hills Police* was still legible on what remained of a small patch stitched above where a badge had been. *T. Dral* was on another patch on the other side of the shirt.

Wade nudged up against a few other zombies, eliciting groans of indifference from the corpses. His one remaining eye was fastened on the faint greenish glow in the distance. The two fast moving figures he'd witnessed earlier had been moving in that same direction, obviously making their way to that area. There was no doubt about it. And so that was where he was heading as well.

The pull was immense and unmistakable. Wade struggled against it; his newfound freewill was being tested to its limits. However, the zombies all around him didn't fare as well. They gravitated toward the unnatural glow without hesitation. Some even shoved others out of their way to move along quicker.

Wade plodded along, trudging through dense brush matted with green fungus. He tapped a rotting hand on his side, creating an uneven but fairly steady rhythm. Eighth note triplets had always been a favorite of his when he was alive. They were the first legitimate beat he ever learned. He was able to apply more of his ideas to eighth note triplets than any other rhythmic format.

The rhythm grew in intensity as frustration welled up inside of him. He hated what he'd become and hated even more what he had done. But he couldn't change any of that now. All he could do was reach the area where the other zombies were going and end it before it was too late.

The green glow reflected off Wade's pallid face as he drew nearer to the spot. Dozens of other zombies filtered about, displaying various stages of decomposition and sporting mixed expressions of relief and frustration. Wade stepped closer and closer to the glow. The flesh on his dead face started to peel, revealing pink-grey tissue underneath. No blood seeped from the wounds.

And then after a strenuous climb up over a fallen tree the size of a small car, he found himself staring into the depression from which the green glow emanated.

*   *   *

Grady Preston did not notice the odd-looking zombie who was watching him with its one remaining eye. He was far too busy flailing around at the outer edge of the Home Growth's light. He couldn't control his arms or legs, or his entire body; it simply gyrated in some obscene mockery of a dance. He felt the snaking fungus multiplying inside. It tickled his organs on its way through his bodily systems, corrupting what was left of his humanity. However, he reveled in the unique power coursing through him. His time was near. His destiny was nearly upon him. And he was going to embrace it.

Grady's eyes darted toward the center of the glow. The shade was changing, transforming to a much deeper hue. A small shape began to form in the vortex. The mass was translucent, lit from within, and it emitted an acrid stench like burning flesh. He leaned in as close as he dared to and squinted his bloodshot eyes. He could discern the shape but couldn't tell what it was. It shimmied back and forth as if alive, reminding him vaguely of a small dog shaking itself dry.

"What are you?" he asked.

A dry hiss streamed out of the glow. It cut through the moans and groans of the undead, adding an even more sinister aspect to the scene. The shape at the center began to twist, contorting to a different shape altogether. It stretched high, nearly escaping the foggy boundaries of the glow, before settling back down into itself. With a raspy chirp, it popped outward to assume its somewhat familiar form: a mushroom.

Grady straightened back up and smiled to himself. He

understood now just what he was meant to do, what he was to become. With a snicker of twisted satisfaction, he plunged straight into the glowing aura. He nestled himself up against the mushroom, and began to tear off slabs of the strange growth and greedily force them into his mouth.

*   *   *

Wade stood on a jutting boulder as he watched the frightening display in front of him. He stared with one eye at the old man who had immersed himself in the green light and now was feeding on something at its center. The scene was eerily lit from within, creating disturbing shadows on the nearby trees and rocks.

The zombie of an elderly lady who was clutching a copy of a Stephen King book in her withered hand shuffled past Wade. She moved up past the brush surrounding the glow and nudged her way past several other zombies who were ringing the green light. Her expression alternated among curiosity, pain, and desire. She watched the old man within the light finish consuming his strange meal and straighten himself upright. A wry grin stretched across her face, a knowing grin full of evil passion and anticipation.

Grady flexed his wiry arms by his side. His bony hands contracted into tight fists and expanded into stretched fingers again. His eyes glimmered with renewed purpose. He scanned the dark figures standing around him, noting how they were all obediently waiting for their destiny to commence.

"Good, good," he mused to the silhouettes circling the light all around him. "We must begin. I shall become a god. A god who rules. A god who sees all."

And then he stood erect. His torso cracked and popped as it began to elongate, stretching upward toward the green-tinged sky.

CHAPTER 28

"How much farther do ya think it is?" Sam asked between gasps for breath. Hs chest heaved under his grimy shirt.

"Can't be too much more," Jerry replied. The image of his little girl's ruined head still clung to his mind…and his conscience. He looked up. Overhead, the sky was gradually drifting into a much darker shade of green. Billowing clouds hung in the cool air, slowly making their way along as if trying to escape the immediate area. The sun began to dip into the purple horizon. The wind ceased altogether.

Jerry thought of it as being in the eye of a hurricane, only worse, for half of whatever was coming had not already passed.

"I don't like the look of this," Sam added nervously. He gestured to the sky. "There are no birds or even any wind," he noted as if Jerry hadn't already noticed himself. His eyes widened and all the color drained from his already pale face. "This is gonna be bad, Jerry. I can feel it."

"Yeah, tell me something I don't already know," Jerry retorted sarcastically. "Now let's keep moving. There's a green light up ahead, past that bend." He pointed toward a narrow pathway which undulated through dense foliage. Large fungus-covered stones were staggered on either side.

Sam nodded while fondling his knife. His hand was so sweaty he had trouble gripping it.

The voice drifted toward them from behind. It was familiar, but so guttural they could hardly understand it. The tone literally oozed malevolence.

"M…must eat. Must obey. Move aside others. Must be a part of new world. An important part. Must eat."

The blood in Jerry's veins froze solid. He knew right away who the moaning voice belonged to. In an instant he whirled around a hundred and eighty degrees and leveled his firearm.

The vacant stare of Ryan glared at the business end of Jerry's pistol. His eyes were nothing more than cloudy orbs reflecting neither humanity nor recognition.

"Must reach growth. N…new world," the fresh corpse drawled through bloody, fungus- stained teeth. Trickles of blackened blood dripped down its sides and were quickly absorbed by sprouting mushrooms.

"Take him out," Sam cried from behind Jerry. "It isn't Ryan! Ryan's dead! We both saw him die!"

Jerry's finger feathered the trigger of the gun. A thin layer of sweat covered his face, mixing with the fear he was feeling.

And then the pistol ignited; it sent a bullet straight into corpse's forehead. Liquefied fungus streamed from the hole and dribbled down the front of its face. With a shaking hand he smeared the unnatural gore across his cheek…and smiled.

More out of instinct than fear Jerry leveled his pistol at the corpse yet again and unloaded three more rounds, all point blank to the head. Instantly three more holes appeared.

Ryan merely laughed, with green fungus-laden spittle spewing from his torn mouth.

Jerry dropped his bag. He only saw a blur as Sam rushed past him. The gleaming blade of his knife sliced through the stagnant air. With one swift, violent motion corpse's head dropped to the forest floor. Strands of rotted tissue trailed down from the reeking stump. The headless body collapsed without a sound.

"I didn't know you had it in you," Jerry confessed to his companion.

"I've found out that I'm capable of quite a bit lately," Sam replied while wiping the gore from the knife. "I hated to do that to him, but I don't think your gun would have done the trick."

Jerry tilted his head in agreement. "Yeah, I guess you're right. I guess you're right. "

The green glow was increasing in its intensity as Jerry and Sam made their way along the increasingly narrowing path. Scores of rancid zombies flanked either side of them, as well as behind; the obvious destination for everyone, alive and dead, was the green light.

"Can you feel it?" Sam asked. His mind was torn between thoughts of what they were about to face and all that he hadn't accomplished in life, most notably reconciling with his father. In a strange sort of way he actually missed the ghostly face of his dad badgering and scolding him at the most inopportune times.

Jerry paused for a moment. He looked at Sam; an onrush of emotion threatened to overtake him.

"Yeah, I feel it too," he mumbled. "It's getting colder the closer we get to that crazy light."

"Colder and smellier," Sam added. "Although that might be from all the living dead around us."

Despite their situation and all they'd been through, both men laughed. It helped to ease the stress and let them think with a clear mind.

The zombies all around Jerry and Sam had increased their movements from a slow, shambling gait to a much quicker and nimble pace. They were nearing their forced destination and were being drawn in like fish on a line. An overweight man dressed in a pair of oily overalls shoved past a pair of twin girls, both of which were missing half their faces. A tall, thin young woman, shattered arms and throat a mass of meaty pulp, stumbled along, bumping into several other dead people. At one point she grimaced in obvious agony when a dangling branch caught the gore-streaked cavity that had been her neck. It tore free a strip of flesh that stretched all the way down to her chest.

"Do you think they can still feel pain?" Sam asked. His eyes were locked on the poor woman. For a moment he thought he recognized her as a customer in the shop at one time or another.

Jerry cradled his pistol so tightly he thought it would break in his hands. "I don't know, but judging by that one's reaction to that branch, I would think so."

The sudden possibility that Stephanie, Wendy, and Seth might not be peacefully distant from their rotting bodies stung him like a hot needle. "But who knows," he added somberly. "Maybe it all depends on the person. Maybe good souls, people who have good hearts, people who have families, people who are loved…" The words trailed off into the surroundings. Jerry doubted their validity but still fought against it. It was just too painful to accept as a possibility.

Both men continued onward. They were getting closer to the green glow, as were the zombies all around them, and with each step the otherworldly fungus increased both in density and in movement.

Sam winced in disgust as the mushrooms snapped at his feet as he trod over them.

"Jerry, this stuff's getting nastier. It's freakin trying to bite me!"

"I know, I know," Jerry replied, narrowly dodging a sinewy growth which stretched over other caps in its effort to reach him; a slick trail of slime graced his shoes, tell-tale evidence of how close the mushrooms had come to him. "But we're getting closer. Just a little bit farther."

Sam grunted in reserved agreement. His head was throbbing and his back was screaming at him, not to mention the smell and the impending situation they were strolling into. All in all it had been a really, really bad day.

Hazy bumps on the horizon loomed in the distance. Jerry strained to make out what they were, (more zombies he guessed), but he only succeeded in giving himself a headache; the lack of sleep was starting to affect his mind as well as his body. He watched the mounds undulate, back and forth, reeking masses of undead, a vast plague of decay waddling along ravines and dense greenery, trudging through streams and around jutting stones, moving with a single forced purpose. A mystery wholly intent on revealing its terrible nature to an unsuspecting world. He just hoped the world would be able to deal with it

Sam paused and rested a hand on Jerry's shoulder. He slowly raised his knife and slipped it beneath the fabric of Jerry's sweaty shirt. "Don't move," he ordered quietly.

Jerry obeyed him despite knowing that standing still in the middle of a zombie apocalypse wasn't exactly a smart thing to do.

Sam lifted the shirt with his blade, and as his suspicions confirmed, gazed in horror at the gestating mass of mushrooms. They had somehow attached themselves without notice and were suckling like newborn babes.

"Trust me, Jerry," Sam urged through clenched teeth. "Don't move a muscle." With the delicacy of a surgeon, he gently slid the blade underneath the largest growth and began to pry it off of Jerry's shoulder.

"Be sure to get all of it," Jerry whispered as he nervously watched the endless sea of zombies move past them.

Sam smiled. "I will. I promise."

Sam worked quickly and yet carefully. He lifted the mushrooms up one at a time, efficiently severing the nearly transparent tendrils from Jerry's flesh.

Jerry felt nothing. "These things must secrete some type of numbing agent when they attach themselves. I don't feel anything."

Sam nodded as he continued his grisly work. "Yeah, I suppose. Kinda like leeches when they suck blood."

A small girl idled past them at that moment. The suddenness of her appearance startled them, as did the fact that the only thing that remained of her head was a jagged piece of her skull cap with a few stands of blonde hair stuck to it by the blood. The piece lay on top of the stump of her neck like some type of grisly hat.

"Hurry it up, will ya!" Jerry said as he carefully stepped aside to let the young zombie pass. He caught a glimpse of a foul green fluid seeping out of the severed end of her Carotid Artery.

Sam looked up from his work. "She couldn't have been more than ten or twelve years old," he somberly mentioned in an off-hand type way. "Reminds me of a girl I had a crush on back in grade school," He paused, "but she had a head."

"Poor kid," Jerry replied, fighting back a new onslaught of painful memories of his family. He was learning that any damage the zombies or the mushrooms could do was nothing compared to the pain of losing loved ones.

"Hold on tight," Sam said through his teeth. "I just have one more to go."

Thick scraping noises rung in Jerry's ears, colliding with the guttural moans from the zombies. Together they made a horrible mix, sounds which definitely did not belong on Earth.

"There, got it!" Sam cried in triumph as he extracted the last remaining growth from Jerry. He held the fungus up, momentarily studying it in the faint light of the forest. The sight up close of the mushroom made his stomach churn.

It was a small pink thing, no larger than a golf ball and was covered in light purple spots. It emitted a faint, but penetrating odor similar to burnt toast and raw sewage. Sam surmised that the stench of the dead all around them contributed to the smell as well. The tiny stalk bent toward him and helplessly brushed against his wrist before it sagged limply. The purple spore prints on its cap began to deepen, darkening to an angry mauve shade, but then retreated back to their original color.

Jerry spun around and his eyes widened.

"Sam! Are you crazy! Drop that thing!"

Sam immediately let the mushroom fall. It fell soundlessly to the forest floor and nestled within a heavy patch of other fungus.

"Sorry," he apologized. "I wasn't thinking."

A sound crept upward from the green light over the bend and settled over the two men like children in the waiting room of a dentist office who hear the drill whine from the other room.

Sam looked over at Jerry. "We have to go toward that, don't we?"

"I'm afraid so," Jerry replied with a grimace. "These zombies are starting to get agitated and aggressive. Our only hope is where that green light is." He looked over toward the glow where dozens of zombies were fighting with each other to get to it. "And we'd better hurry. I don't think we have too much time left."

CHAPTER 29

Grace shoved Cliff ahead of her. Rows upon rows of mushrooms snapped at his feet as he passed, but were unable to get a bite on him. He guessed it was Grace herself that did not allow them total access to him, she somehow exerted control over the growths.

"Why didn't you tell me?" he whimpered as they threaded their way toward the green otherworldly glow. "We can all get along. We're a race of peace and love." He knew his corny words were falling on deaf ears, especially since Grace didn't seem to have ears anymore; only stubbed, oily knobs greasy with green fungus were on the sides of her head by then. He tried not to look back at her, but what was ahead of him was even more disturbing, and undoubtedly more lethal.

Grady was oblivious to both Grace and Cliff. His body was molding itself into an entirely new form of life the likes of which had never been seen before on Earth. And he would also make sure it would never be seen again.

His newly anointed cohorts swarmed around the glow, each vying for prominence. Rotted faces leered viciously from all sides, visages smeared with a combination of knowledge of their purpose and a blissful ignorance. They sensed what they'd been drawn there for but still did not completely understand it.

Grady didn't care however. He was charged with power far beyond what mere mortals, living or dead, could possibly understand. With immense strength he inserted a pale, gnarled finger into the center of his forehead and slit the flesh downward, effectively cleaving his face wide open. Glistening green meat, punctuated by the yawning hole of his toothless mouth and the now sightless orbs of his eyeballs, peaked out from the opening. Within seconds the still human part of his flesh slid off of the pulsating mass of shuddering alien growth that he had become.

Cliff tried to close his eyes as he was forced to approach the abomination in the light. The acrid stench of diseased flesh being simmered in the green embers of the Home Growth stung his nostrils. His stomach seized repeatedly, on the verge of voiding itself of whatever remained in it.

Grace continually nudged Cliff closer and closer to the monstrosity, which was gradually thinning as it grew in height; seven, ten, fourteen feet high it reached, threatening to extend even higher, above the treetops themselves. She said nothing while prodding her unfortunate captive forward.

"Grace, please," Cliff pleaded. "It doesn't have to be like this." He felt the bile rise in his parched throat as he brushed against an armless zombie still wearing the soiled remnants of a pinstriped suit and loud tie. "I... I thought you were my friend."

Grace paused momentarily from her efforts. A faint glow of remorse streaked across what was left of her face, briefly reflecting in the light of the Home Growth. But then her visage grew cold again and promptly extinguished any traces of remorse or compassion. Again she pushed Cliff forward.

The zombies ringed the green light and the dark figure within it. Old, young, male, female, large, small. The undead displayed a wide spectrum of physical attributes, all grotesquely connected by the state of their various condition: dead. They swayed before the emerald maw and the opaque silhouette writhing in it. Their dead skin began to slough off, slipping to the ground to puddle in thick syrupy remains which reeked of death...and something else: freedom.

Grady was not recognizable as a human being anymore. His body was being reborn, surpassing the boundaries that any man could endure: his arms had withered drastically, fusing to his sides; his legs melted into one grotesque pillar of alien flesh; his head elongated as he grew; all in all he was an abomination unlike anything God had ever intended. Higher and higher he stretched. Fifteen feet, eighteen feet, twenty feet. He twisted back and forth, reaching for the swirling chaos of the sky. His foul, corrupt servitors pooled far below him, basking in the malevolent light of his greatness. To him they were merely ants consigned to do his bidding. But he also knew they were something more. They were a part of him.

CHAPTER 30

Jerry noticed it first. The towering figure was before them, reaching upward at least twenty feet. It hardly resembled a human, a black mass somehow lit from within with a cold green glow. It resembled a throbbing artery pulsating with life. This clearly distinguished it from neighboring trees.

"What in God's name is that?" Sam cried as he dodged yet another zombie. The fifty-something man in torn blue jeans and a Detroit Tigers jersey swiped at him as he stumbled along in his hurried attempt to reach the green light. "Is that....is that alive?"

The black vortex that had been Grady Preston crackled and bubbled as it grew. Squirming groups of zombies churned in violent turmoil at the black thing's base. A blustering gale split the darkened sky. A sharp, bright lightening forked downward toward the impending collapse of Humanity. The storm was descending on the unfortunate population of Toals Creek and Highland Hills, and debris-strewn wastelands were the only thing it promised.

"I may only be guessing, but I think we've made it," Jerry said; a nervous smile crossed his face.

"Yeah, I think you may be right," Sam agreed. His face was pale with sweat. "By the way," he added tersely, "what exactly are we supposed to do?"

"I know what I'm gonna do," Jerry growled. There was a flicker of revenge glinting in his eyes. "I'm gonna stop this mess before it gets any worse. Those things took my family, and I aim to get back to my last kid in one piece. And if I do go down, I'm taking that thing with me."

"So you don't know either?"

"No, not really. I'm making it up as I go along."

"Great. Just great."

"Yeah, tell me about it."

Sam chuckled. "I don't think the weapons we have will do much good against that thing." He gestured toward the still rising black figure.

Jerry nodded, not taking his eyes off of the horrid spectacle. "We might as well throw sticks and stones at it." He glanced down at his handgun. Without another word, he tucked it back into his pocket. Looking around, he recognized several zombies from town. The sliver of hope he clung to withered with each familiar dead face he noticed.

Pat and Janice Arron were clumped together like rotted strands of taffy, their infected blood and tissue streaked with green. Despite the absurdity of it, Jerry found himself wondering if Pat had driven his beloved Camaro to this pre-ordained spot. Louise Sampson and her son Jack, the former stereotypical picture of a loving mother and son, were now nothing more than dripping entrails loosely held together by a hateful irrationality and threaded with a malevolent hunger. And Officers Dral and Szothern, clammering along like all the rest of the dead, oblivious, or simply not caring anymore about their loyalty to the badge, about the oath they took to protect and serve, about their own families or friends. Only their foul destination shone on their dead faces.

Jerry almost called out to the former officer in a vain hope that being peacekeepers they might still retain a trace of their humanity. But one baleful glance in his direction from the remains of Officer Dral was all it took to suppress the urge.

The black figure was starting to expand, both in height and girth. It swelled and churned, smacking its way toward a greater mass. The air around it distorted as its chemical balance was disrupted. Thick tendrils dripped from its sides, momentarily giving it an alien, octopod shape, before being swallowed by festering ulcers resembling glowing bedsores.

Jerry and Sam cautiously crawled up to the edge of the depression. The zombies all around them continued along, only a few sporadically glanced in their direction.

"I think we're running out of time," Sam whispered. He was flat on his belly next to Jerry, his knife pushing into his side and his bladder full, threatening to void itself if he didn't take steps to alleviate it. The mushrooms were thin beneath them, and fortunately for them, weren't attacking.

"Tell me something I don't know," Jerry replied with a grimace. "We're gonna have to apply *Double Q* to this mess."

Sam stopped in mid-crawl.

"Say what?"

"*Double Q*. It stands for quick and quiet, although I don't think being quiet will help much."

A look of confusion creased Sam's brow. "If you say so."

Jerry smiled grimly and started to move forward again. He could feel the mushrooms pulsating beneath him, and although relieved that they weren't attacking, he was still sickened by the feeling. The fact that just a short time ago he was a happy family man burned his mind with the severity of contrast to what he now was. He'd been reduced to a widower slicked with grief and dirt, shimmying along flat on his stomach in the middle of some God-forsaken woods, approaching a growing, alien monstrosity obviously intent on world domination.

And then yet another thunderbolt of anguish speared Jerry's heart. For there, directly in the hub of the maelstrom, in the shadow of the towering abomination, was a figure writhing in a glorified mockery of a dance. Its thin arms swayed in constant motion, circling high above its head as the cold green glow bathed it in its unwholesomeness.

Jerry strained forward and rubbed his eyes, as if that simple physical gesture could erase what he was seeing.

"You okay?" Sam asked

Jerry fought back another breakdown. "Yeah," he mumbled. "It's just someone I see. A woman zombie missing her left hand."

CHAPTER 31

The torrent of damp misery gushing from the rising black figure, which had been Mr. Grady Preston at one time, spun in all directions. Green showered the multitude of zombies standing nearby, coating everything in an infected open wound of impending doom. The apocalypse was near, and it was funneling its destruction through Grady.

Higher and higher the black figure rose. Eventually it skirted the treetops before poking through the highest branches, and up into the churning tempest of the sky. Lightning split the heavens, thunder boomed in the air, the temperature cooled, spikes of ice dotted the trees.

Far below, deep down in the forest, scores of undead milled around, gathering near the Home Growth and its cold glow of unnatural green light. Among their number, Cliff stood, not more than ten feet from the hub of pulsating alien life. His swollen eyes were locked on the towering black mass in front of him. Behind him, Grace had rooted herself into the ground; steaming roots festered around her feet. Her distorted body was propped up by the strange malignant growths.

Grace smiled; tiny shards of green fungus pulsated in the hole that had been her mouth. She didn't speak and Cliff found himself wondering if it were due to the way her mouth was distorted or the fact that she was simply reveling in the sheer terror she was causing.

Cliff turned back to face the growing monstrosity towering before him. It was easily forty feet tall, maybe more, and the cold clammy aura of death and decay emanating from it was overpowering and absolute. The stench of the zombies assaulted Cliff's nose and stung his eyes. Their raspy moans twisted his gut.

"You will be used," Grace scowled from behind him.

"Used? Used for what?"

"For food."

And with one violent shove, she pushed Cliff directly into the swollen mass of the dead. They overwhelmed him with their jagged teeth and grasping arms, tearing into him as a starved lion would a rare steak.

Cliff's life flashed before his eyes as his flesh was gouged by desiccated hands. A shrill cry slipped from his bloodied mouth and uselessly drifted upward to be swallowed by the black abomination of Grady Preston. And with one final moan of pain, Cliff slipped from life to death…and then to undeath.

Sinewy strands of fungus seethed within the glowing embers of the zombies' faces. Their bodies were splotched with a veritable maze of green growth; mushrooms sprouted everywhere. They were starting to coalesce. Bubbles of a milky substance laced with blood and fungus formed and popped. Engorged faces swooned in pained ecstasy.

The growths then began to direct the zombies' bodies. They steered them into the seething cauldron of black death that had been Grady Preston. They resembled grotesque marionettes with mushrooms moving their limbs instead of strings.

The zombies surged forward into the towering pillar; the corpse of Cliff was at the head of the movement. Geraldine Baxter fell into the black mess, her copy of the *The Stand* incinerating into a wisp of gray ash. Mrs. Ether from Toals Creek waddled forward, not a single thought of what the repairs to her Ford would cost her was in her fungus-encrusted head. Al Moser bumped his way past the others. His age was not a factor to him anymore, nor was the fact that most of his midsection was missing, hallowed out like a ripened cantaloupe. Despite having virtually no vital organs left in his body, he still displayed considerable strength and dexterity, easily pushing aside several other corpses in his bid to reach the black swirling chaos.

One after another, the dead slid into the black pillar. The green glow at its base continued to radiate is unnatural light, but in a gradually lessoning way. The glow was feeding the black figure, and in turn was being fed by the countless dead lumbering into it. Their bloodless flesh stripped from their bodies by the cold fire of green light, the zombies poured onward, swelling the black mass with each pound of death they offered.

Wade found himself concealed behind a large tree. The thick girth of the trunk afforded him a good deal of protection, but he couldn't help but wonder just why he was hiding. Was he afraid? And if so, of what? He was dead after all, just another zombie in a vast sea of corpses.

And then it hit him. Could it be because he still retained some traces of his humanity? And was it due to his freedom of thought? His independence, his free will?

With his one remaining eye, Wade watched the nightmarish spectacle unfold from the relative safety of his hiding spot. Several other zombies passed by him and growled in a threatening manner. Perhaps they resented his ability to resist the calling of the green light.

The black figure continued to rise, spewing out large quantities of mushrooms and fungus-coated slabs of itself, which in turn, stuck fast to the hordes of lumbering zombies, further directing their corpses into the Home Growth.

Wade darted behind the tree, narrowly dodging the incoming fungus. It slapped against the bark and dripped down the trunk, leaving thin, vertical lines of residue. At the top of the black thing which had been Grady Preston, an open wound split the substance, exposing fibrous strands within. These strands wove together to form a bulbous head that stretched up and out of the glistening cavity. The shape smoothed to a rough orb before gradually elongating at its top, and the bottom two circular depressions formed in the upper half, followed by a long vertical bridge directly below them. This bridge flattened itself somewhat, culminating in a widening hole which grew in size rapidly. Within seconds, it had opened a full five feet across. Huge sabers of jagged teeth peeked out from the newly-formed maw.

The forest froze as the black thing's head tilted down to survey its new kingdom.

CHAPTER 32

Double Q didn't have the same effect, the same promise of safety as it carried before. The urge to call out to Stephanie was difficult for Jerry to resist, so much so that he had to cover his mouth with his own hand.

"Man, I can't hold it anymore!" Sam suddenly blurted out. "I'm sorry, Jerry." And with a stifled grunt of relief, he voided himself as he lay on his belly. Warm urine seeped into his clothes and soaked his clammy skin.

"Never mind that," Jerry whispered through his fingers. "We have to get closer to that thing before it gets any bigger." His eyes instinctively darted back to Stephanie. "We have to stop it before...before she goes into..."

Sam, relieved from his release, caught sight of what Jerry was staring at. He felt obligated to say something, but he couldn't find the words. So he let it go.

Jerry finally broke his gaze and promptly stood up. He suddenly didn't care anymore about his own safety. He'd watched his family die and the world threatened by some killer fungus. In the grand scheme of things, he simply didn't matter anymore. He'd sacrifice his life if he had to, willingly, without hesitation, if it could somehow bring him closer to Stephanie, and Seth, and Wendy.

But the responsibility he had to Martin, his remaining child, forced him to adopt a new outlook, one that required, that demanded, he do everything in his power to survive, and to insure the survival of the human race if he could.

Sam watched his companion with a mixture of fear and wonder. He would have opted for a more stealthy approach to the situation, but quickly realized he had little choice but to follow.

"Sometimes it's best to go into something blindly," Jerry announced. "Trial and error, improvisation, making it up as you go along." He looked back at Sam; an uneasy grin was on his face. "Besides, I don't exactly know what to do or what will stop that thing. But I do know if we do nothing, it's not gonna go away on its own.

More than anything, I want to get to my son, but I feel I owe it to the rest of my family to at least try something."

Sam fought back tears. Suddenly he missed his parents. "Sounds good to me," he said with a smile. "Now let's go and save the world."

The swollen black form swayed from side to side, seething in its own power, rending the very sky itself in its bid to grow. A thick myriad of tendrils formed on its sides and blindly groped in the stale air for anything or anyone to latch onto. Nearby trees received the brunt of its force, bending to its destructive whims, and splintering under the assault. Branches and leaves fell to the forest floor in a shower of obliteration.

As Jerry and Sam drew closer to the monstrosity, the smell grew more pungent and their courage thinned. Thoughts occurred to both men. It wouldn't be too tough to simply turn around and leave the area; the zombies all around them apparently were more interested in reaching their forced destination. Jerry could head down to Ohio and find Martin. Hopefully the infection hadn't spread that far. And Sam could scurry back to his simple, eventless life, passing his days fixing cars in Feeter's Automobile Repair Haven and trying to ignore his father's nagging face. One had more to live for, more at stake so to speak, but both still had a life he missed.

Jerry looked at Sam, and Sam back at Jerry. Each read the other's face, saw the fear and doubt harbored there, noticed the toll the devastation had taken on them. Simultaneously, they both nodded, and turning to face their terrible adversary, combined their courageous resolve and moved forward toward their destiny.

A mere thirty feet separated Jerry and Sam from Grady. The black thing's tentacles, recently grown and engorged with supernatural strength, easily had enough length to simply stretch out and swat them into oblivion, but didn't. Instead, the arms concentrated on coercing the hapless throngs of zombies into its mass.

"Looks like some twisted mother cuddling with her babes," Sam said.

"Yeah, well, we're gonna just have to break up this little family picnic," Jerry retorted with a sneer. "I have a gut feeling that our best weapon will be the one thing we have that it doesn't have."

"Oh yeah? What's that?"

Jerry looked Sam straight in the eye. A fire burned there, a smoldering flame of determination. A flame that had enough and wasn't going to take any more.

"Our humanity."

"Humanity?"

"That's right. Our humanity. Our life essence. What makes us tick." Jerry paused for a moment, willing himself to believe in his own words. "Don't you see? That's what separates us from them. We live. We breathe." Again he paused. He remembered the origin of what he was about to say. "We.....love."

Sam smiled. "I see what you're saying. Maybe that thing can only grow if it's fed with things that are already dead."

"That's how I see it," Jerry agreed.

"So all we need to do is feed it something alive, something that still has a soul." A flash of doubt crossed Sam's face. "So who's it gonna be?"

Jerry laughed despite himself. He felt relieved that after all he'd been through, he still could laugh, even if it was in such a dangerous situation.

"Haven't figured that part out just yet. I guess we'll go on in and see what happens."

*   *   *

Wade watched the two men wind their way through the throngs of trembling zombies. It puzzled him that neither wielded any type of weapon. Their very movements seemed unprepared, not stealthy or powerful or with purpose, but without a plan to implement that purpose. In life he always was an organized person. Everything had its place, every day had an agenda. So to see the two men advance on the black monstrosity the way they were confused him.

It also prompted him to move.

Wade stepped forward, leaving the protective barrier of the tree behind. The zombies all around him continued to plunge forward. Their expressions were anxious, as if being engulfed by the towering abomination would somehow bestow life on them again. Their past memories, and loves, and fears were lost like a cobweb in a dust storm, and Wade knew that they would never get them back.

And then somewhere deep inside, he felt a new urge, a desire to help and preserve human life. He had achieved his freedom through sheer willpower and now he was going to use it to help the two men. How, he wasn't sure, but he was determined to try.

Wade staggered forward. The other dead ignored him. Did they sense one like themselves? Or were they perhaps simply focusing on reaching the black thing and achieving their desire for life? The woods were literally flooded with dead, and it wasn't easy to get past them, but Wade plodded onward, eventually reaching the rim of the Home Growth. His seeping face glistened within the cold green light.

Jerry and Sam didn't notice Wade. To them he was merely another member of the walking dead. To them he simply meshed into the stinking vastness of rotting flesh and missing limbs.

"So what do you think?" Sam asked, his eyes glued to the throbbing black pillar before them.

Jerry studied the thing for a moment. He managed to put his fear aside and examine the monstrosity from a totally objective viewpoint. It might be the only way they'd be able to understand the creature. It might be the only way they could defeat it.

"I think it knows we're here."

Sam couldn't help but notice the zombies which were circling him and Jerry. They drew nearer with every movement, their stench settling over all around them.

"How do you know that?"

Jerry didn't answer. Instead, he merely pointed upward toward the top of the black mass. There, roughly seventy feet up, was the newly formed head of the creature. It had what passed for its eyes securely and solely on Sam and Jerry; they reflected seething hatred mixed with curiosity. It knew they were there, but it didn't know why.

Why living beings would deliberately advance into its obviously powerful grasp it couldn't understand. With a scant gesture, it motioned to its undead army to subdue the men, to ready them for ingestion.

Jerry's eyes were torn between the towering thing before him and the reeking dead surrounding him and Sam.

"Well, now what?" Sam asked. He was also switching his gaze between the black thing and the zombies. His hand rested on the handle of his knife inside his pocket.

"Clear your mind of any fear," Jerry instructed. "Humanity should show no fear. Mankind has built an advanced civilization from people taking risks. We should use their accomplishments as our strength."

Sam nodded, but his gut churned as he struggled to control his fear. After all, it wasn't every day that someone was surrounded by decaying zombies while standing before a seventy-foot monster. But that's just what he was doing.

The black thing shivered with some type of excitement. Ropy tendrils threaded their way down its sides as it continued to rise. With each dead body it consumed, it steadily grew. Seventy-five feet…eighty feet…eighty-five feet. Its grotesque form passed the treetops, sloshing its way up to the turbulent skies above and beyond.

Jerry and Sam were pushed closer and closer to the base of the creature, the frigid aura from it stung their senses. Blistered zombies nudged them forward. Cold, decayed hands bit into their backs. Hollow eyes bore into their souls. Neither man resisted. They harbored inside knowledge, information that the dead didn't know about, that the quivering mass before them didn't know. And it would allow them to defeat their nemesis.

Or at least they hoped so because they were not only betting their own lives that it would work, they also knew very well that mankind's fate rested in their hands as well.

CHAPTER 33

"They must be killed first!" the horrid form of Grace Preston howled to the zombies. "Sever their breath from their foul bodies!"

Jerry and Sam turned to look at the shrieking woman. She bore little resemblance to a human, other than her bipedal body and two arms flailing about what they guessed was her head. Protruding from her torso was a myriad of dull black appendages, which seemed to become agitated by the living beings nearby. She undulated back and forth, as if she couldn't decide whether or not to grow or stay the same size.

"Stop them! Kill them now!" she screamed.

Several zombies lunged forward eagerly, their trembling hands grasping for the two men.

Jerry fought them off, brandishing his hands and arms like weapons. He pummeled the dead in their faces, his fists sinking into the palpable flesh like a hammer striking bread dough. Some fell back, stunned by the violent display, while others weren't deterred as easily.

Sam stood directly behind Jerry, shielding himself as best he could from the onslaught. There were zombies coming up behind and on either side of him, their intent was clearly etched on their mottled faces. He knew that he would have to act, and quickly.

The faint image of his father's face materialized in front of Sam. It wore an expression of concern. Sam was unaccustomed to seeing concern in his father's face. And for a moment, just a brief moment in time, he could have sworn his father really was there.

What's the matter boy? Do you doubt your own senses?

Sam narrowly dodged a small boy who swatted at him with fleshless fingers. The kid zombie quickly backed away after its attack. Its blank eyes resembled a shark's, soulless and a slave to its hunger.

Sam's father lowered his eyes. A look of genuine sorrow flashed across his face. *Sam,* he mumbled. *I never told you…I always meant to but didn't…*

Sam was touched by the heartfelt display but didn't have the luxury of listening to a warm father-to-son discussion.

"What?"

I've always been proud of you, although I didn't show it. I know you have the strength and courage to do what's right. His eyes narrowed and his lips curled into a wide grin. *Go into the darkness, Boy. Go into its soul before they kill you. Go!* And then the face faded into nothingness.

Sam understood what his father had said. His humanity, his soul, his life essence would be enough to combat the thing before them. It had to be; it was all they had.

He moved out from behind Jerry, and shuffled forward, bypassing the row of dead sliding into the black monstrosity. He stood before the thing, feeling the cold radiating from it, resisting its powers, reaching for him, trying to draw him into the hands of its undead minions. He knew what he had to do, and for the first time in his life, he felt he had a purpose. For once he felt like he really could make a difference.

"We gotta save the world," Sam announced. "Jerry, you keep them off me, and I'll take care of the rest."

Jerry was too busy to fully grasp what his companion was saying. A particularly large man and woman zombie (possibly husband and wife in life) had him flanked and were clawing at his head. The dead man was very much overweight, although his obvious lack of food intake after his death caused considerable sagging of his body. His torso literally dripped off his large frame. His supposed wife was in even worse shape. She listed to her left due to a missing foot and ankle, and was split open down the middle, revealing God's complicated network of veins and organs, all of which were compromised by fungal infection. With each movement she made, her innards trembled, threatening to spill onto the ground. All in all they made the perfect couple, two people together in life and swollen in death. Jerry also noticed one other thing about the pair before he cleaved their heads open: they were holding hands.

The figure approached Jerry from the far side of the Home Growth. It was slender, almost shapely, and moved among the zombies quickly, never taking its eyes off of Jerry.

"Hello, Honey. Did you miss me?"

The voice struck Jerry like a locomotive, barreling over any remaining traces of courage he still had. He stared at his wife, watching her lithe body beckoning to him with its false, dangerous promises of becoming a husband and wife again. Green and red gore stained her face and neck, and her arms were riddled with open sores. Trickles of green fungus dripped from every single one.

Happy memories of their former life together flooded into Jerry's mind, nearly incapacitating him where he stood.

"There's someone else here who misses you honey. Seth? Come out, Son. Your father wants to see you now."

Jerry's fifteen year-old son waddled out from behind the corpse of his mother. He looked no different from that fateful night when he and his younger sister had attacked their father, other than the obvious fact that his skin was so pale it showed every vein in his thin, adolescent body.

"Hey Dad," the cadaver said. The voice was laden with antagonistic sarcasm. "Mom said you killed Wendy, blew her little head off." Feral eyes drilled into Jerry's. "But don't worry about it. She's all right. In fact, she's right here."

Jerry's heart then tore for the third time as the gory remains of his daughter hopped out from behind a row of zombies. What was left of her head shook when Jerry screamed as loud as he could.

Without giving himself time to hesitate Jerry yanked his gun from his pocket and fired two rounds into the little corpse's chest. The force of the shots sent the girl stumbling backwards and into the black squirming mass of alien life.

In a brief second she was gone.

Jerry launched another bullet (his last) directly into his dead son's gut and watched with a broken heart as Seth vanished into the quivering monstrosity behind him as well.

Stephanie raged as she catapulted herself at her husband. The gory stump where her left hand used to be flailed above her seething face.

"Why don't you join me now, Honey?" she growled as she

lunged for Jerry. "We can go into the Master together and soon we will be gods! But first I have to kill you!"

Jerry reared back and narrowly dodged his wife. The stench nearly knocked him out, but he held his ground, and with one viscous blow leveled Stephanie's corpse with the butt of his pistol. She reeled backward and collided with two young male zombies directly behind her. Together, all three of them plunged into the icy depths of the black pillar.

The anguish Jerry felt was compounded by something he noticed before the mother of his three children was swallowed whole: there was a flash of remorse on her pitted face. It was barely evident, but it was there. Despite all she had done she still loved her husband. Even while (or perhaps because of) being pulled to her death, she still maintained a part of her humanity, the part that separates mankind from the rest of the animal kingdom: Love.

The dead were falling all over themselves in their frenzied efforts to reach Jerry and Sam. Rotting limbs tangled with other rotting limbs. Shredded faces mashed into one another. Twisted feet tripped over other twisted feet. The huge black figure that had been Grady Preston shimmied back and forth as it continued to surge to even greater heights. The churning mass of dead at its base appeared as no more than quivering ants to it, wallowing tadpoles in a pond observed indifferently by a young boy.

The black pillar watched from its lofty vantage point. It felt the sustenance its minions served to it. Each dead body was a full entrée, a jolt of energy which it consumed with unbridled relish, absorbing it into its future, its destiny. The world was coming into its view with every movement it made. It would tear the sky wide open and spew its poisonous fungal brethren into the atmosphere. It would populate the planet with its breath, a homing beacon for others near or far. Its bloated form sloshed from side to side. A vile cacophony coiled around the forest and all those near it, plunging the world into its cesspool of gloom.

A lone sparrow flew by at that moment, coming dangerously close to the black thing's head. It spun through the tainted air, oblivious to the world-shattering carnage far below. Wind raced past it as it glided along.

The black thing trembled as it attempted to dodge the bird. It did not want the strange air-born creature; it wasn't dead. The sparrow, although only a small, inconsequential animal, still possessed a rudimentary soul, a desire to live, to mate. It hadn't been prepared properly. Its blood still coursed through its small feathered body.

The bird flapped its wings a few times, and angling its beak upward, soared higher into the turbulent sky. It had sensed the evil and hunger of the black thing and decided it wanted no part of it. Fortunately for the sparrow it possessed the anatomical devices to allow it flee unharmed.

A greasy spray of liquefied fungal matter jetted from the reeking maw of the black thing. The mist shot with uncanny precision and quickly engulfed the hapless sparrow before it could escape. The bird dropped, falling to the forest floor far below, becoming nothing more than another dark blot in the swirling landscape of the dead.

CHAPTER 34

Wade stood still as he watched all the terrible events before him unfold. The two living men who were fighting with the dead were completely unaware of his presence. He was merely another zombie in their eyes. Just another nameless victim in the vast plague of the undead.

Wade observed the two men who were a mismatched pair to say the least. He kept his distance from them, suppressing the envy he felt about their lives. His desire to help them was fractured by his desire for nourishment, even though he didn't really need to eat. He'd grown strong-willed, being able to differentiate between right and wrong, and he knew that helping them was the right thing to do.

Sam stepped out from Jerry's shadow. A slew of undead reached for him, but found he was a difficult target; he was quick and nimble. His mind was singularly focused on his mission. No doubt clouded his thoughts. No hesitation hindered his movements.

Grace threaded her way toward the two men, systematically shoving aside less mobile zombies in the process. Bulbous green mushrooms dotted her grotesque body. She clenched her hands several times, drawing forth partially liquefied fungus, which she began to hurl at Sam.

"Foul beasts!" she cried. "This rock upon which you dwell shall be ours!"

Sam dodged the flying fungus, although barely. A thick glob of the stuff grazed his left shoulder, sending searing streaks of white-hot pain through his body. He could feel the probing tendrils snaking into his arms and legs, corrupting his vital organs and draining what strength he still had. He felt weak, his legs buckling beneath the weight of his body.

Jerry couldn't help; he was held fast by two male zombies. One's head had completely rotted away, exposing the nub of its vertebrae, which was pressed up near Jerry's mouth. Frothy green fungus bubbled as it strove to infect and ultimately kill Jerry, thus preparing his body for absorption.

Sam collapsed where he stood. His strength ebbed away with each passing moment, nudging him ever closer to his fate, which he feared, also intertwined with the fate of mankind.

"J…Jerry. You have to help me," he moaned. But he knew Jerry was as helpless as he was.

I know you have it in you, Son, his father's voice said calmly. *Ever since you were a little boy you've had strength you never dreamed of. I've known it all along, Son. Now prove it to yourself. You have what it takes to do what's right. I know you do.*

"Dad? Is that you again?"

The smiling face materialized in front of him. It nodded its head.

Sam clenched his teeth and dug out his knife. The blade gleamed in his hand as he studied it. Sweat mingled with the coating of grime covering his face.

Would he be able to do what needed to be done? He had to. There simply was no choice in the matter.

He raised the knife to his shoulder, and in one quick motion, cleanly sliced off the top layer of infected skin.

"Son of a…"

I knew you could do it, Son, his father's face said while nodding in approval. *I knew you had it in you.*

The flap of diseased flesh dropped to the ground with a wet thud. Sam grimaced in disgust as he kicked dirt and leaves over it.

Jerry, still held fast by the two zombies, managed to free an arm and immediately swung a sharp right to the face of the dead man who still had a face. His fist sunk into the rotting tissue easily, cleaving the zombie's head wide open. Liquefied brain matter and throbbing fungus poured out.

More zombies advanced on him: dead children (one still in the shredded remains of a soiled diaper); a young housewife still in her stained apron; a tiny, elderly man emancipated further by undeath, and the worst one of all…Grace Preston.

"Behind him, you fools!" she shouted at the dead. "Hold him for me!"

Jerry felt his knees shake at Grace's words. He watched, mesmerized by the things approaching him. The cavity of endless black stretched wider and wider as it came toward him; green blotches of poisonous mushrooms rimmed its undulating edges. He could feel the cold grasp of the black thing behind him. It yearned for his body, for his life, but it was incapable of acquiring it on its own. It needed the help of its minions.

Sam spun around and carefully took aim with his knife. He ignored the bright, crippling pain from his shoulder and flung the blade with all his might dead center into Grace's midsection. An ear-splitting howl of agony ripped through the air when the bloodstained steel struck its target.

"Sam?" Jerry muttered while still grappling with the zombies. "We gotta do something, and fast." He was keeping a small girl zombie at bay with his foot. She repeatedly snapped at his shoe, attempting to fasten her broken teeth onto it.

Sam watched his knife slip into Grace's deformed body; it was as if she swallowed it whole. Reacting quickly he turned and flung himself at the growing black thing before he thought better of it. His father had told him he had an inner strength, and that was good enough for him. He'd accomplish something in his life. He'd make sure of it.

But Sam didn't see the enormous figure until it was too late. Before he knew what had happened, he found himself gasping for breath within the grip of a muscular six and a half foot tall zombie.

"You ain't going anywhere," the vast creature announced. "Or not at least until you're ready to." And with those foreboding words, the dead man increased the pressure in Sam's neck. The veins in his thick arms pulsed, despite no blood flowing through them.

Precious air dwindled for Sam. His eyes rolled back in his head as his mind fogged over with vague recollections of his childhood. His life was flashing before his eyes ,and he was powerless to stop it.

In his delusional realm, Sam drifted from misty thought to misty thought. His mother's kind face swayed within the gentle maelstrom, occasionally colliding with images of other friends and family members. Animated shorts slipped into rambling, inconsequential episodes. Each represented both good and bad times, happy and sorrowful, and all were underscored with the nagging suspicions that something else was at work, something dark and foreboding in its intent.

The horrid face of the enormous zombie was the first thing Sam saw when he plunged back to reality. His throat was still in the dead man's hands and he could literally feel his soul being squeezed dry. His eyes bulged and his face turned blue.

"Kill him! Kill him now!" Grace screamed as she hobbled around the towering zombie. "Kill him and cast him into the void."

And then Sam's world went black. His brain, deprived of the oxygen it needed to properly function, shut down, sending a dense sheet of night over everything he knew. In a way he welcomed it.

CHAPTER 35

The black thing towered over its kingdom. It continued to expand due to the legions of undead feeding its massive bulk; it swelled larger and larger as it gorged itself on the bodies of its slaves. Inside, it could feel the cyclopean cogs churning, greased with the poisonous slurry of the fungus and the foul viscera from the dead. It was a well-oiled machine that was growing, literally, into its destiny.

Yet deep down within its core was a faint, barely resonant flicker of human life. The tiny speck thrummed quietly, curling in unto itself, and unfolding again and again in a vain attempt to retain any trace of its humanity that it could.

Grady Preston fostered some remorse despite his best efforts to suppress it. He was, after all, a human being, born of flesh and blood, raised by a father and a mother, taught right from wrong. He'd grown up believing in God and all that He stood for. In his mind there was a Heaven and Hell, and he even entertained the notion that there was a purgatory which resided in all its desolate glory somewhere in between the two.

And just where he was now he wasn't quite sure.

His mission had been clear to him ever since Grace had supposedly died. He'd known it all along, simply waiting for a sign to start him on his journey. And it had finally come, but what had happened to him was beyond anything he could have ever dreamed of.

The black thing focused its attention on the flurry of activity at its base. In addition to the dead plunging their bodies into its growing form, it noticed the two humans who were being accosted by zombies. It saw them thrash about wildly. One appeared to be securely within the grip of a particularly large zombie. He violently wiggled back and forth as if having a bad dream.

And the black thing saw Grace as well. She had changed drastically, a far cry from the dark-haired beauty it vaguely remembered, but it was her. It was sure of it.

Grady watched her from within his prison. She stood behind a large zombie, gesturing for the dead to kill the living. Her shouts were like music to his ears. Her voice had changed, become more vicious, more pronounced in its severity, but it still opened up a plethora of memories in him. He would have smiled at that moment if he could have. He was delighted that Grace was still alive. She hadn't died in the fire after all. After the fire, he'd spent years of his life living alone, not knowing, or caring, what was going to happen to him. After he'd lost his wife, nothing seemed to matter to him anymore, or at least until he'd found the mushroom.

Grady felt his control slipping away. The thing he had become, in which he was imprisoned in, was shoving him aside as it grew in both size and power. He was merely another gear in the machine, another blood vessel within its body.

The black thing surged upward, clipping trees and swallowing the sky. It convulsed as it carved the woods with its enormous bulk. A tremble singed its form, like a balloon being filled with too much air. It was threatening to pop. A chorus of howls drifted up toward its summit, adding to the slick cacophony of its growth.

Deep inside of it, bubbles of frothing spores built up. Plugged with the alien bile of other worlds, the tower distended yet further, resembling a bloated earthworm writhing in a rainstorm. The time was nearing for it to splash the world with its spawn.

*   *   *

Wade felt the urge growing inside of him; he couldn't deny it any longer. And so with a snort of defiance, he pushed his way forward, efficiently shoving aside the ever-growing ranks of the other undead. He had one destination in mind: the huge zombie strangling one of the humans.

The creature was much larger than he was, and Wade fought back a slight trace of fear when he approached the monster.

"This is for making me kill my family!" he bellowed to the other dead man. The voice was guttural and raspy due to the gelatinous condition of his vocal chords, but the meaning was clear.

Bending down and grasping a mushroom-covered stone, he

stood up and reared the rock behind his head just as the big zombie spun around to see who was threatening him. And with one savage arc, Wade flung the rock directly at his adversary's head.

The stone landed squarely between the beast's eyes, splitting the head open like an eggshell. The big corpse reeled from the blow, stunned as its face was cleaved open, revealing a sickening potpourri of rotting brain matter and seeping fungus.

Sam landed with a thud when his attacker collapsed into a motionless heap. The sudden influx of air revived him, and the entirety of his situation came crashing back into his mind.

"J…Jerry?"

The dark form towered over him, side -stepping jostling zombies to reach him.

"Secure him!" the figure shouted. "Prepare him!"

At their leader's orders, several of the dead gathered around Sam. They were in various stages of decay, and each sported terrible wounds ranging from missing limbs to exposed internal organs. All sneered and grumbled at their intended victim.

Sam struggled to get to his feet, but his head still felt light. He sagged back to the ground repeatedly, disoriented and weak.

Come on, Son. Get up. Get up. I know you can do it. I know you have it in you. You're the one destined to save the world.

"I... I'm trying. But my head. I can't see straight."

Cold hands clasped around Sam's arms, roughly hoisting him up. The stench was overpowering, which in a way helped revive him somewhat. He shook his head to clear it and glanced from side to side.

"You must be prepared now!" Grace shrieked. "Now!"

It seemed like some sort of bad dream to Sam. One minute he was being attacked by the clawing blows of the zombies, and the next minute he was free from their assaults, whirling around and around in his own private universe. He sensed he was moving, but which way or how was beyond his comprehension. But he was still alive, that much he knew, and that's all that really mattered.

He fell further and further into his world as strange, irrelevant thoughts drifted about: would he be able to go to work tomorrow? After all, his boss was dead and the shop trashed. And how would he be able to afford getting his car fixed? And was Mrs. Ether going to pick up her Ford soon? He wondered if Tim was all right. And his folks. God how he missed them now, even the hazy illusion of his dad.

For the first time since the zombies attacked, Sam felt safe, nestled comfortably within his own thoughts, wrapped up in the false security, firmly believing that it had all been some type of bad dream.

A young woman zombie put up a struggle, but lacking parts of both her arms, she was no match for Wade. She went down quickly. Another, a middle-aged man still sporting his *Hi, my name is Randy* button on the tattered shreds of his navy blue grocery store uniform, managed to get Wade in a crude headlock, but fell to a sharply placed kick in the groin. Thick, green residue splattered across the ground from the dead man. Two small zombie boys, who couldn't have been more than nine or ten years old when they died, wound up as a congealed mass of broken limbs and blood-streaked faces when Wade was through with them.

Other zombies broke down before the superior force of Wade's strength as well. His free will had somehow given him added dimensions of power. Blood still within his wasting body coagulated into something beyond what he was, beyond what any of the other zombies were.

Sam was sprawled out, a spent pile of flesh and bone. His mind wandered peaceful plains far away from the carnage his body was trapped in. He felt his heart beating wildly in his chest, but still he was calm. He was searching for his own private utopia.

Wade approached the still body at his feet and gazed down at it; he felt pity and remorse for it. The man was still alive, although barely, so Wade bent down and scooped him up in his arms.

"Kill them! Kill them!" Grace shouted through a twisting hole for a mouth. She danced up and down in a fury, her body an infectious ruin bent on the destruction of all around her.

Wade plodded forward on his dead feet. Sam was motionless in his grasp. Zombies clawed and bit him, attempting to snatch the living one from him, and they groaned in frustration at their failure to do so.

Grace herself had resorted to hurling sticks and stones. In a sense she knew she was helpless, as were the others. Wade could not be stopped, would not be stopped. He had a will of his own, a semblance of humanity, and he knew right from wrong. And since he was already dead he wasn't overly concerned with his own safety.

Grace charged at Wade, snorting obscenities and howling in rage. Wade glanced at her for a second, and then while gripping Sam tightly against his chest, plunged straight into the black gloom of the Home Growth.

CHAPTER 36

The sun was starting to peek through the thick dark clouds, casting its warming rays on the still landscape below. The bright beams of sunlight carved slicing strokes through the dull gloom of the sky, effectively releasing the forest from the ominous grip of the zombie apocalypse.

A light breeze picked up from the north, bringing with it the fresh scent of clean air and a new start. The wind washed over the trees and through the foliage, touching every stone, every leaf, cleansed the forest from the infection it had endured. The stench that had permeated every crevice in the woods gradually diminished, replaced by Mother Nature's scent.

The residue from the fungus dissipated rapidly. Faint traces of the other- worldly growth remained for a short time, but the combined sunshine and warm breeze diluted the pathogen considerably. Within the short span of an hour, perhaps two, nature had taken back what had originally belonged to it: God's gift of a peaceful ecosystem, unhampered by the dead or malevolent beings bent on the Earth's destruction. There were no mushrooms sprouting up from the ground. No fruiting bodies stretching into the sky, reaching for any passerby to infest. No sickening green tint other than Mother Nature's own unique colors.

Jerry pulled himself up off the ground. He felt like he had an anvil resting on his head, one that was on fire no less. His mind gradually conformed back to its original state, and although scarred from his ordeal, the fact that they had quite literally saved the world assuaged the pain somewhat.

They?

With his head swimming in painful disorientation, he'd almost forgotten about Sam, the man who helped him through this terrible holocaust. The man who had sacrificed himself, ultimately destroying the towering black growth, which as far as Jerry could tell, was preparing to burst open, spilling God knows what across the world.

A single tear welled up in Jerry's eye as he surveyed the

carnage. Some trees lay flattened, skeletal reminders of what had occurred in the forest. Some were completely obliterated altogether. Others were still standing, although their limbs bore telltale signs of severe damage. Huge patches of barren ground spotted the forest floor, trampled into nothingness by the mindless footfalls of the undead. Nature had taken a beating, and Jerry found himself wondering if it would ever be able to recover.

His gaze locked in on the black wound on the ground off to his left. The area was huge (approximately thirty feet in diameter) and coated in a fine layer of soot-like material. The earth was depressed significantly within it (nearly two feet deep in some places), and traces of a milky green substance splotched several portions of the spot. As a whole it was a terrible sight, a mottled abyss of ghastly proportions. Jerry obviously surmised that is was all that remained of the black form that had swallowed Sam.

But why had it died? Why did Sam's sacrifice stop it from completing its mission? And what had happened to all the zombies?

These questions spun around in Jerry's head, mixing with the confusion, exhaustion, and relief already there. He was tired, and he still sported various injuries, but fortunately, none were too serious; they were mostly superficial. His eyes were swollen from the stench of the dead and every part of his body ached, but he was alive and that was all that mattered, or at least for the moment.

Sam was gone, as were the dead and the towering black mass. Something in Sam's body must have reacted somehow with it. Perhaps, as Jerry had said earlier, it was his soul, his humanity that did the trick. The alien fungus, or whatever it was, simply couldn't adapt itself to the concept of its food having a life of its own, its own soul. It needed mindless dead for nourishment. Nothing more. Nothing less. But all that was inconsequential now. Water under the bridge so to speak.

Jerry scanned the area; there were no signs of any bodies or mushrooms. In fact, all seemed normal save for the black spot on the ground and the damaged trees and foliage. Thoughts of Martin flashed across his mind. How glad he would be to see him again. Stephanie was dead. Seth was dead. Wendy was dead. Most of his life had been ripped away, but God had saw fit to leave him one thing: Martin.

Each and every step hurt like hell, but Jerry didn't mind. Every movement he made took him further away from the nightmare and that much closer to Martin. Civilization beckoned from its safe, comfortable perch, laden with living human beings and clean, fresh air to breathe.

God, fresh air. What a welcome thing that would be. It had been so long since his lungs enjoyed a good cleansing breath.

The woods hindered Jerry's steps, seemingly slapping at his heels with a reserved malevolence. He trod on though, doing his best to ignore any threats, real or imagined. His body and mind had been put through the meat grinder, but in certain ways he felt revived from it. *Whatever doesn't kill you only makes you stronger*, or something like that.

A pair of eyes watched Jerry as he trudged along through the brush. They focused on his every step, his every movement, intent on studying him, curious as to his destination. The eyes were swollen, with brown puffy bags beneath them, but they still were more than capable of clear sight.

Jerry was unaware that he was being watched; thoughts of reuniting with Martin filled his mind, and his current surroundings placed a distant second. A Mack truck could have driven past him and he probably wouldn't have noticed it.

The eyes continued following Jerry as he came nearer and nearer to them. From their vantage point, they had a clear view of the lone man walking through the woods.

"Hello? Can you help me? I'm hurt."

Jerry stopped instantly when he heard the voice. The words were like silk to his ears. It seemed as if he hadn't heard another person's voice in years. He fingered his pistol, gently drawing it out of his pocket and leveled it in the general direction of the voice. His hand was shaking as the owner of the voice stepped out from behind a large fallen tree trunk.

She was beautiful, even though half of her delicate face was obscured by ragged strands of black hair. Jerry could still see her eyes, piercing green pools of warm sorrow; they reflected tragedy, and not just from their immediate surroundings, but a far more personal type. He lost himself in those eyes, falling further than he ever thought he was capable of.

The girl smiled at him. She straightened up and brushed herself off, taking extra care not to disturb anything near her. Her blouse was torn in spots, most noticeably across her stomach area, and the jeans she had on were stained dark, most likely from blood. A few purple black bruises dotted her small arms.

"My name is Nora," she said quietly. Her delicate hands dangled at her sides.

Jerry felt tongue-tied. Feelings awoke in him that he immediately felt ashamed of but couldn't deny. In a far away section of his mind he envisioned Stephanie's heart breaking.

"Jerry. Jerry Ott," he muttered.

The girl smiled and looked down at her feet like a shy schoolgirl. She had no weapons or any supplies, and Jerry found himself wondering how she had managed to survive. Hoards of rotting zombies, alien fungus, towering pillars of black flailing about, engulfing anything organic nearby. The sheer magnitude of the impossible dangers she must have faced was immense.

Her arms hung at her sides, giving her an even greater look of attractive innocence, an attribute that was not unnoticed by Jerry. She vaguely reminded him of a girl he'd had a crush on in high school. There were so many questions he wanted to ask her, but he could hardly manage a coherent thought. Still, above it all, one indisputable fact remained: she had survived.

"Are you from around here?" Jerry asked quietly. He felt his stomach spawn scores of butterflies.

"I'm from Toals Creek. Born there back a ways."

Jerry laughed. "That's near Highland Hills," he stated with smile. "That's where I'm from, Highland Hills that is."

"I've heard of that place."

"Really?"

"Oh yes. My uncle owned a car repair shop and I would go there sometimes to pick up or order parts for his business."

"Small world."

Nora brushed her hair away from her face, revealing elliptical green irises. Jerry felt himself being pulled away from the terror he had endured, from all the horrible images still clinging to his mind, and into those eyes. Peace resided there, and suddenly all he craved was to lose himself in them.

"We should get to know each other better," Nora suddenly blurted out, seemingly startled at her own words. "I like you. I like you a lot. I really think we can be friends. Very, very good friends."

Jerry was taken aback by the boldness of her words. He quickly decided to steer the awkward conversation in a different direction.

"But how did you manage to survive? I mean, that is you must have seen the zombies."

"My family was killed by zombies. I hid out in a bookstore in town. Acorn Books it was called. I used to go there all the time with my mom. They had all kinds of rare and antique books; some stuff was from the 1500s. The owner knew me by name. He was a real nice man too." A wave of sadness washed over her pretty face. "I suspect the zombies got to him as well. I doubt he's still alive." She continued as they began to walk. "Anyway, I stayed out of sight, huddling in the horror section, fittingly enough. Several times some dead people came near the store, but I guess they couldn't sniff me out through the smell of all those musty old books. Did you ever notice how book stores have that certain smell to them? Most of the time it was single zombies, but a few times there were big groups of them."

"That's amazing," Jerry said, "although I suspect the zombies were forced away from the store by the alien fungus. I saw it happen to many of them myself. My...my wife... I mean a woman named Stephanie attacked me in my house and then left for no reason. None whatsoever. I could have been killed right then and there. Right in my own house."

Jerry felt the tapping pain of his memories. He saw the images of his life fading away in his mind's eye, becoming more and more obscured with each passing moment. And worse still, a new life was gradually replacing it, and he was completely helpless to stop it.

Nora stopped walking and turned to face Jerry. Her eyes bore into his, drilling her thoughts, her beliefs into his mind. "Are you all right?" she asked.

Jerry shook his head to clear his mind. The remaining memories of his wife and children, his house, his job, all remnants of his previous life floated away like so much dust in a breeze. Nora was what mattered to him now. She was all there ever was. All there ever would be. There was nothing before he'd met her, only a vast plain of oblivion that stretched out behind him like a desert.

"I... I'm fine," he stuttered, wholly unaware of his own childish mannerisms.

Nora grinned. "Good. Now that we're together I need to make sure you're safe and sound."

"Ahh...okay. We're together. Safe and sound."

She nodded. "That's right Jerry. Safe and sound. Now I have a gift for you. It's a very special gift, one that cannot be replaced. And it's for you and you alone. Do you understand?"

As Jerry nodded Nora withdrew a small object from her cleavage. The package was no larger than a tennis ball and was wrapped in green cloth that was stained with moisture. A faint but pungent aroma drifted up from it.

"Here. Go ahead, take it."

She handed the object to him.

Jerry grasped it in shaking hands and gazed down at his curious prize. Without hesitation he removed the wrapping.

"It's for you," Nora repeated. Her expression was tinged with a dark, feral undertone. Green hues curled around her features. Her visage reflected her true origins, although subtly.

Jerry looked at the small pink mushroom in his hands. It had bright white gills and a faint spore print of lavender dots on its sizable cap. A shiver of excitement rushed through him when the growth began to tremble, thin streams of translucent slime dripping from its cap and stalk.

"You must keep it with you at all times," Nora said. Her voice was stern and unwavering, like a teacher instructing a pupil. "Promise me you will. Promise me."

"I will," Jerry replied sheepishly. "I promise I will. At all times."

"Good. It will let you know when it's ready for you."

Jerry nodded and wrapped the mushroom back up, tucking it into his pocket. He managed a weak smile.

The couple held hands as they sauntered away toward the misty hills on the horizon. The sky had cleared considerably, coating the landscape in warm sunshine, and the trees which still stood swayed with the gentle breeze. And behind them, skirting their disappearing footprints in the brush, were countless residual traces of green fungal growth.

The mushrooms waited.

Read Rick McQuiston's next terrifying novel:

Where Things Might Walk

Due out early 2012 from Many Midnights Publications.

ABOUT THE AUTHOR

Rick McQuiston has been a life-long fan of anything even remotely related to horror. He vividly recalls seeing *Jaws,* and *Alien* when he was a kid, and immediately became engrossed in the dark genre.

To date, he has written over 125 short stories, and four novellas. He's had over 250 publications in several countries, including numerous anthologies, and has published five collections: *Many Midnights*, *Chills by Candlelight, Beneath the Moonlight, As Mean as the Night,* and *Rick McQuiston's Cold Dark Tales,* as well as one book of novellas, *Private Nightmares.* He also edited and contributed to an anthology of Michigan-based authors, *Michigan Madmen.* All are available on Lulu.com, Amazon.com, and his website (*many-midnights.webs.com*).

He is a guest author at Memphis Junior High School each year, as well as local libraries, and book, art shows. Currently, he's hard at work on his second novel (*Where Things Might Walk*), adapting an earlier tale into a novella, and countless more short stories, all of which haunt his every waking moment with their insistences to be let out.

Visit him at his website, or email him at Many_Midnights@yahoo.com.